LOVING TWO

Darkisle 2

Cassandra Pierce

POLYAMOUR

Siren Publishing, Inc.
www.SirenPublishing.com

A SIREN PUBLISHING BOOK
IMPRINT: PolyAmour

LOVING TWO VAMPIRES
Copyright © 2011 by Cassandra Pierce

ISBN-10: 1-61034-244-5
ISBN-13: 978-1-61034-244-5

First Printing: January 2011

Cover design by Jinger Heaston
All cover art and logo copyright © 2011 by Siren Publishing, Inc.

ALL RIGHTS RESERVED: This literary work may not be reproduced or transmitted in any form or by any means, including electronic or photographic reproduction, in whole or in part, without express written permission.

All characters and events in this book are fictitious. Any resemblance to actual persons living or dead is strictly coincidental.

Printed in the U.S.A.

PUBLISHER
Siren Publishing, Inc.
www.SirenPublishing.com

DEDICATION

I'd like to dedicate this one to Rachel Clark, a fabulous Siren author and the best Beta Reader anyone could hope for; and also to the other Rachael, for listening and responding so patiently to the crazy ideas I spew after I tank up on cappuccino.

LOVING TWO VAMPIRES

Darkisle 2

CASSANDRA PIERCE
Copyright © 2011

Chapter 1

"It's called fieldwork, Joel," Lindsay assured her worried cousin. "People do it every day. I'll be fine. Stop being such a cop."

"Well, I am a cop." His voice began to crackle over the cell phone as her car strayed farther from the beaten path. "Or a deputy, at least. And I don't like it—civilians going undercover. The world's a dangerous place these days. You've lived in Boston long enough to know that."

Lindsay hitched her shoulder higher and pressed the phone tighter against her ear. "I've also lived there long enough to know how to protect myself."

"Fair enough, but I'd feel better if you told me where you were."

"I can't. I gave my word. If you knew what I had to go through to get this address..."

"That makes me even more nervous."

Lindsay sighed. Joel, a year older, had appointed himself her protector twenty years earlier when she'd come to live with her aunt and uncle as a foster child. She doubted his attitude would change now, especially while he carried a badge and gun.

"Look, I just called to tell you I'll be incommunicado for a few days. I don't want you going all goofy and calling in the state police or something. You know me. I'm not a risk-taker. Never have been."

"Well, keep your phone with you and preprogram my number. I'm here if you need me."

Another burst of static invaded the line, and the connection faded and died. A moment later, the GPS on her dashboard failed, too. That came as no surprise, since the roads she took existed outside common knowledge, but it might have creeped out someone more superstitious.

Her journey had taken her far, far north of Darkisle, the grimy seaside town she'd grown up in. Ten years earlier, she'd escaped its dull confines and headed south to Boston and an education that helped her shake off the narrow morality and small-mindedness of her hometown. Now, ironically, she'd traveled back up the coast to complete that journey.

The quest had taken her almost to the Canadian border, through fragile covered bridges and over pitted, unpaved roads banked on each side by immense trees and menacing rock formations.

More than once, she began to worry that her goal didn't exist. The loss of satellite and phone signals reinforced that concern.

Then, suddenly, somehow, she was there.

The club wasn't what she had expected. Brightly lit, the architecture a shimmer of fused metal and glass, its sleek façade jutted from a cluster of dark, massive trees in a perfect synthesis of ultramodern and primeval. A few patrons clustered outside the entrance, waiting to pass a pair of bouncers stationed in front. Soon she would be part of that same eager crowd, seeking entrance to a world few knew of and even fewer experienced.

She had to convince herself that she belonged among them. If she could accomplish that, Lindsay figured, she could persuade the people around her, too.

A pale, sunken-eyed valet motioned her to the curb of the circular driveway the moment she pulled close enough. She stepped out gingerly. In her effort to look the part, she'd donned tighter clothes than she'd ever worn in her life, mostly consisting of leather and laces, with a top cut so low that her nipples threatened to pop free every time she moved and knee-high boots that flared over crimson tights. Thick, studded wristbands and a high-collared cape completed her costume.

Testing her theory, she flicked the cape strategically open when she handed over her keys. The valet gawked at her, but his expression seemed more wistful than inhospitable. Wordlessly, he climbed into the driver's seat she'd vacated.

Though she'd spent months preparing for this moment, Lindsay watched with a stab of apprehension as her only means of transportation glided away into the darkness.

Still, she couldn't turn back. She'd come too far and invested too much in this project. A little luck—and some Oscar-worthy acting on her part—and she'd return to the city with all the data she needed.

The broad-shouldered, black-suited sentry outside the double glass doors met her eyes boldly, searching her face for any sign of fear or hesitancy. Affecting a self-assured swagger, she pushed through and swept past him with the briefest acknowledgment. In return, he offered her a brief nod of acceptance.

In-group behavior, she thought. A good sign.

She'd made it inside.

The space she entered resembled many urban nightclubs, including some perfectly innocuous ones she'd visited in Boston over the years. The light was dim, with occasional flickers from a rotating strobe on the ceiling, and an industrial beat throbbed in the background. The usual assortment of patrons leaned against the walls and lounged at tables strewn around the circular bar in the center of the room. At least she'd pegged the dress code. The majority of the women were wearing Goth outfits like hers, while the men favored leather pants and sleeveless shirts. Chains and intricate tattoos abounded.

As she stood observing the scene, an attractive African-American woman in a short silver dress approached her with a tray of what appeared to be shot glasses full of pink, yellow, and green fruit juice.

"Welcome to Purgatory," the woman said, expecting her to take one of the odd-looking concoctions. After pretending to weigh the three choices, Lindsay picked up the pink one and hoped she was correct to assume it was complimentary.

"I haven't seen you here before," the server said.

Lindsay assumed a haughty air. "An associate recommended this place. I'm curious to know whether it can live up to my expectations."

"I hope so." The woman smiled and moved on with her tray. Lindsay exhaled in relief. Another test passed. Lifting the shot glass, she sniffed at the contents. Fruity, with no hint of alcohol. A house specialty, perhaps? When she raised her eyes again, she saw that many of her fellow patrons were nursing the same drink.

It would serve as a prop, then. Another sign that she belonged. Clinging to it, she moved deeper into the room. She didn't know where she was heading, but she kept her expression determined and her strides purposeful. As she walked, the heavy gazes of strangers slid along her body like groping hands.

One man in particular made his interest plain. Though he wasn't holding a drink, he was leaning back against the bar, resting his well-muscled frame on his elbows. Instead of some trendy faux-medieval costume, he wore a simple outfit of tight slacks and a pale, open-collared shirt. His dark eyes blatantly scanned her up and down, then drifted upward again, his mouth half-curved in a smirk. He didn't bother to look away when Lindsay paused and stared back at him.

Hastily she diverted her attention to a woman about her age, seated at the bar, who seemed a promising source of information.

"Good crowd tonight," Lindsay said casually, sliding onto the vacant stool beside her. "Last time I was here, the place seemed deserted."

The woman turned and stared as if Lindsay had spoken to her in a foreign language. Lindsay, in turn, was taken aback by the woman's multiple nose and lip rings, dark streaks of makeup, and skin as pale and transparent as skim milk.

"Are you okay?" Lindsay asked with sudden concern. She couldn't identify what drug the woman was under the influence of, but her vacant expression and her obvious weakness suggested something pretty strong.

Abruptly, the woman rose, abandoning her drink on the counter, and moved off into the crowd.

Lindsay got to her feet as well, preparing to follow, but the press of bodies around the bar stopped her. She didn't need to glance back to know that the man she'd spotted earlier now stood right behind her.

"She won't talk to you," he purred, leaning forward until the words caressed her ear. "She didn't come here for conversation any more than you did. This early in the evening, it's all about competition."

Lindsay's mostly-exposed skin prickled as though his intensity had sparked a mild electrical current. Just then she spotted the pale woman again, passing through a doorway set into the wall just behind the bar. Several people had clustered around it, watching a few others slip through. That was where the real action took place, Lindsay suspected.

Time to start her research in earnest.

Pretending she hadn't heard the man's comment, she slipped through the crowd and stepped into the next room. As the door slammed shut again, she heard a few murmurs of admiration and encouragement. That struck her as odd, but she had no time to dwell on it.

If the outer room had seemed uncomfortably close to a typical city bar scene, the space Lindsay now found herself in resembled nothing she'd ever experienced before. Here, the lighting was so muted that it barely qualified as such. Thick blue smoke swirled around her, bringing with it strange smells—clove cigarettes, exotic incense, human sweat, and pheromones. Lindsay stood immobile, trying to adjust to the gloom, while silhouetted figures squeezed past her.

Just ahead, a mass of people danced in place. Despite the feverish beat thudding from a row of gigantic speakers, the dancers swiveled their hips and shoulders languidly, moving in a kind of daze. Though she'd anticipated a certain degree of lawlessness, Lindsay felt a slight shock when she realized that some of them wore nothing but a few strands of jewelry.

She stumbled ahead, avoiding the shuffling dancers, struggling to absorb every sight, smell, and sound without appearing too curious. When she got to the back of the room, however, she was unable to conceal an expression of utter astonishment.

On a platform in the corner, a naked man posed in front of a large wooden "X," his wrists and ankles spread out and tied to its frame. Three women hovered around him, bending and bobbing their heads over various portions of his anatomy. Lindsay assumed they were putting on some kind of sex show, until she realized that each of the women held tiny daggers, which they were using to make shallow cuts on the man's exposed flesh. With every push of the knife, he moaned and writhed in apparent enjoyment. Meanwhile, the women licked away the fresh blood as soon as it trickled from his wounds.

"Is he all right?" Lindsay hadn't meant to speak out loud, but imagining such scenes and actually watching one proved to be two very different things. She wasn't nearly as prepared to bridge the gap as she'd imagined.

"Perfectly." That same silky voice rumbled against her flesh again, startling her. "He offers himself every week or so when his supply is replenished. It is completely voluntary, infinitely pleasurable to him, and much safer than it looks."

He was standing so near to her that the thick ridge of his thigh, not to mention the bulge of his zipper, pressed against the curve of her half-covered rear end. She turned her head to find the dark-haired man from the bar. Up close, he was even more striking, with eyes so dark that the irises appeared black in the room's strange lighting. A wave of even blacker hair swept back from his forehead, the thick, inky mane curling down behind his ears.

This time, his proximity didn't set her on edge. Quite the reverse. The sheer power of his presence made her feel secure for the first time since she'd walked in here.

"His supply of blood, you mean," she replied in a shaky voice.

He tilted his head in agreement.

"How much will they take?"

"Enough to slake their thirst, but not enough to harm him. I'm sure you know that a healthy individual can lose quite a bit without experiencing anything more serious than temporary weakness."

His tone held a hint of challenge, and Lindsay's stomach knotted. Had he seen through her ruse? If so, no wonder all her carefully cultivated bravado, so foreign to her true nature, had melted the moment she found herself confronted by his strong-jawed face and ruthless eyes.

"Of course I do," she shot back, deciding to use the opportunity to do some research. "I just…wasn't familiar with that technique. I mean, knives? Don't vampires use their teeth?"

His lips parted with humor. It wasn't exactly a smile. "Don't worry. Before the night is over, they will."

"On him?" She swallowed and turned back to the man on the scaffolding. His erection curved upward, swelling with each swipe of the women's tiny blades. Lindsay had once studied the phenomenon of people who took pleasure from cutting their own skin. She'd never understood the appeal of self-mutilation, but even that seemed almost normal compared to what she was watching now.

"Doubtful. He has his role to play. But there are plenty of other willing volunteers in this room." His brows lifted suggestively. After all, she reflected, she was passing herself off as one of those volunteers. Surely he didn't expect her to strip down and get up on stage herself?

Just then, the crowd shifted, some spectators apparently becoming bored with the display. Lindsay found herself separated from him, borne away on a surging human tide. Her relief at escaping his inquiries proved short-lived, however. Another man immediately took his place.

Her new companion provided a stark contrast to his predecessor. His appearance alone unnerved and disgusted her. This man's long, unkempt gray hair slithered to the shoulders of an equally ragged shirt. The pungent odor of blood and decay rose from his skin.

For the first time since entering Purgatory, Lindsay experienced a flash of genuine fear. Stubbornly, she pushed it away. She wasn't about to be intimidated by a regular guy with a delusion—and an apparent aversion to bathing.

She gasped as the man's rough-skinned arm slid around her and locked under her breasts. Her back collided with his bony chest at the same time his clammy fingers pushed aside her skimpy clothing and encircled the hard bud of her nipple. Icy breath fluttered over the back of her neck. Sheer revulsion paralyzed her.

"You look like a tasty morsel," the man growled. At least she thought that was what he said. His words sounded garbled somehow, as though he were speaking an odd, backward form of English resembling Pig Latin.

"No!" she protested, struggling to liberate herself. "Let me go!"

The arm squeezed tighter, cutting off her breath. Forced into silence, panic rising, she concentrated on using her nails, heels, and shoulders to loosen his hold. Nothing had the slightest effect.

Her blows became weaker as the pressure on her lungs intensified. Then, unexpectedly, she found herself stumbling free.

As her vision swam back into focus, she found that the tall, dark-haired man in the light shirt had returned. He and her attacker were squaring off, hands and feet spread, muscles rippling with anger. Much stranger, though, was the sound they were both making…a low, feral growl, like jungle animals clashing over a fresh kill.

Lindsay's head was spinning, thanks to her momentary loss of air, but the second voice boomed above the grinding techno beat.

"Back off. I saw her first."

In response, the foul creature who had grabbed her hissed and bared his teeth. Lindsay went weak again at the sight of his spiky, discolored fangs.

Fake, she reassured herself, even as an icy sweat erupted down the middle of her back. There were underground dentists and body modders who would file people's teeth to create the illusion of vampirism. Still, whatever his status as a card-carrying member of club undead, he would have bitten her, she felt sure.

The crowd of onlookers quickly transferred their attention from the man on the platform and gathered to watch the unfolding battle instead. A middle-aged woman with an elaborate glitter-laced hairstyle blocked Lindsay's view, but she heard another round of roaring, a few more incomprehensible phrases, and the shuffling sounds of the combatants circling each other.

Lindsay managed to duck and step to her left just in time to see the man who had grabbed her go down on his knees, his wrists imprisoned in her rescuer's stony fingers. Sputtering like a trapped beast, he thrashed his head from side to side, as unable to escape as she had been only moments ago.

"You may be older than I," the dark-haired man asserted, "but I am stronger. Don't cross me again, or you will be pining for the moon for another two hundred years or more."

He pushed off hard, sending his opponent sprawling on the floor. The spectators murmured with disappointment as the lanky-haired man lurched to his feet, hid his blotchy face with his hands, and scuttled away. No one followed him, but the crowd dispersed soon after, leaving Lindsay standing alone, terrified and embarrassed in equal parts.

"You're supposed to consent before they do such things," the man said with disgust as he approached her. He looked down at his palms, scowled, and wiped them on the thighs of his pants. "You didn't welcome his attentions, did you?"

"No. It all happened so fast. He just—came out of nowhere."

"Glad to hear it. He is a creature not to be trusted."

"I kind of got that impression."

"He's a product of the Middle Ages, so he hasn't quite mastered the concept of showing respect for women. Chivalry was by no means as universal as the legends would have us believe. Then he lay imprisoned in a tomb for over two centuries, and it drove him a little mad. I almost pity him. Almost."

Lindsay gaped at him. "How do you know that?"

"Because I helped put him there, of course." He folded his arms and stared at her until she found herself getting lightheaded again. "This is your first time here."

It hadn't been a question, and she saw no point in denying it. "Yes."

"Name?"

"Lindsay Tanner." She hadn't meant to reveal her last name, or at least not her real one. Somehow, it rose to her lips as if she had no control over her own speech. The assault must have shaken her more than she'd realized. "Uh…yours?"

"Caine Waldram." He reached out and grasped her hand. The coldness of his skin sent a shiver up her arm and straight to her nipples. Her own face suffused with heat as the front of her skimpy outfit stretched outward to form twin points. Caine's smile expanded along with the garment.

"An interesting name," she said in an effort to distract him.

He shrugged. "People took Biblical names seriously when and where I was born. Either my parents had a strange sense of humor or they had a premonition about the sort of man I would become."

"The Biblical Caine was cursed, you mean."

"He also murdered his brother. Fortunately, I remained an only child."

Though he was no longer touching her, she shivered again. "Well, you seem like a fine man to me. After all, you just saved me from that disgusting man…and from myself, I suppose."

"I did what was necessary. I'll speak to management later and get our ill-mannered friend barred." He shrugged again, distracted. His gaze swept the room behind her. She was tempted to turn around, but resisted the urge. For some reason, she couldn't tear her attention away from him. He captivated her in a way the objective researcher in her found unsettling.

"Good idea."

His smoldering gaze swung around again and pinned her. Whether a trick of the lighting or not, his eyes still appeared entirely black—perhaps like those of his Old Testament namesake. "And aside from that, are you enjoying yourself tonight? Do you like Purgatory?"

No doubt he expected her to comment on the pun, so she ignored it. "It's…interesting."

"I can see why you would say that. You didn't come here looking for companionship, like most everyone else. Nevertheless, you look lonely. I'm not sure you even realize it."

In fact, Lindsay didn't consider herself lonely, even though her determination to earn a series of academic degrees and soon, hopefully, start a career, had made her personal life unsatisfactory at times. "There's a difference between being alone and lonely," she protested.

"I didn't just mean tonight." He lifted his hand and turned it palm upward to indicate a spot across the room. This time, she pivoted on her heel and looked in the direction he indicated.

"Now there's a man who needs companionship," Caine went on, his arm still raised. "Gabriel Blackstone is another very old acquaintance of mine, but he happens to be one you can trust. And I know as well as I know my own name that he's lonely. So go."

His hand dropped to her shoulder, and he nudged her so subtly that Lindsay was moving forward before she even realized it. She didn't need to glance back to know Caine had vanished again.

A tall blond man stood in the spot Caine had directed her toward, holding a tall metal goblet to his chest. His chin tilted up, and his gaze remained vacant, as though he were trying to lose himself in the strobe lights and music.

Even though he scared her a little, she found Caine Waldram handsome. She couldn't deny that.

But Gabriel Blackstone was, simply, the most beautiful man she had ever seen.

Chapter 2

She approached him, her strides slow but deliberate. Gabriel lifted his goblet and drained its contents. He let the empty vessel hang at his side, loosely rolling it in his long, delicate fingers.

Lindsay spent a moment drinking in the sight of him—loose hair falling to the top of his shoulders, tight v-necked shirt hugging his narrow chest, muscled arms exposed by pushed-up sleeves. His posture was taut, almost defensive. She half-expected him to turn from her. But he didn't.

"Hello, Gabriel. I'm Lindsay," she ventured. "We have a mutual friend."

He nodded, pursing his lips. The gold stubble around them glistened with moisture. She found herself mesmerized by the supple fullness of his mouth. "Caine."

She detected weariness in his voice. "You've known him a long time, he says."

"Only about a hundred and fifty years." His face registered amusement at Lindsay's dismayed expression. "So, are you enjoying the show?"

He waved his empty goblet toward the man on the platform. The three women who had been lapping at his wounds had moved on to seek other diversions, leaving him to writhe and moan by himself. Sweat and blood glistened on his bare skin, and his swollen cock stabbed the air every time he arced his hips.

As a researcher, she knew better than to engage emotionally with the subject of a study. Yet, somehow, she found herself getting caught up in the spectacle of this place, not to mention these strange appetites. Though bound and naked, the man in front of her exuded not helplessness and indignity, but a yearning so intense it became pleasurable in itself. His slack face, half-closed eyes, and straining erection spoke of an arousal pure enough to transform not only him, but those around him.

Including her.

She shivered when Gabriel leaned closer, his loose hair brushing her shoulder. His question hadn't been an idle attempt at making conversation, she realized. He awaited her answer.

"It...it isn't quite what I expected," she blurted.

"No? Why are you here, then?"

"I wanted to see this place firsthand. I was curious."

"Curiosity kills more than cats." His hand moved too fast for her eyes to follow. He tipped back her chin and leveled a penetrating stare at her. Though his fingertips were cool, Lindsay's entire body flushed with heat. "But you are more than an ordinary cat. A pantheress, perhaps, looking to be tamed."

"No. Not at all."

"I can sense things about you that you're probably not even aware of."

"Impossible," she said, though her words didn't sound convincing. "You know nothing about me."

"Caine sent you to talk to me. That in itself suggests certain characteristics. The rest I can fill in myself."

Before she had a chance to reply, his arm encircled her waist and dragged her against him. When she caught her breath, Lindsay looked up at him, startled. He was staring straight ahead, still pinning her to his side. She followed his line of vision and understood the reason for his peculiar behavior.

A group of rowdy men and women swept by them, talking loudly. One of the women extended her arm as if to knock Lindsay to the floor on her way past. Only Gabriel's quick action had spared her certain humiliation.

The woman and her friends glanced at her contemptuously as they sailed along. Their smirking mouths were smeared with something dark and thick. Their cold laughter hung in the air. It echoed deep in Lindsay's mind even after they'd moved on.

"No manners at all." Gabriel shook his head and set her back on her feet. "They don't seem to realize that driving the human guests away won't leave much fun for any of us."

"The human guests?" Apparently Gabriel was as deep into his role-playing as everyone else here. Had he, too, abandoned all sense of reality for the tacit sadism of this odd subculture? She hoped not, and for purely selfish reasons.

"That's sort of the point of venues like Purgatory. To bring our two worlds together. Right?"

"Well…yes. Of course."

Though she was no longer in any danger of being knocked over, his hand still rested on the small of her back, keeping her close. "Tell me again why you came here. You may be curious, but there's more. Exactly what are you looking for?"

She met his challenge with a bold tilt of her chin. "You said you could read me. So do it."

The ghost of a smile lifted his mouth. Again, his hand moved much faster than her eyes. His fingertips came to rest against the underside of her jaw. They stroked her skin lightly as he eased her head farther back. Their gazes locked.

"You want to prove something," he decided. "Not only to me, but to yourself. And others who have accompanied you only in your mind. They may never know that you have passed their test…but you will know. That matters to you."

Her lips parted in surprise. Granted, he was fishing for a vulnerable spot, performing what skeptics called a cold reading. The fact that he had found her own spot so quickly, though, threw her off balance for a moment.

"You don't want someone to dominate you," he continued. "You're far too headstrong for that. But you do want someone who can push you far enough to let you lose yourself in pleasure. In the old days, society did its best to convince women that they were incapable of lust. Now we've corrected that tragic misconception, but some women still try to deny it. Like you."

His cool fingers began to massage the flesh around her throat, sending a delicious current shimmying down her spine. An unexpected burst of heat pooled in her center. She caught herself breathing faster.

"I don't deny that I'm capable of lust," she replied, careful to keep her voice level and her tone neutral. "It's a primal instinct, a biological imperative. However, I do believe there's a time and a place for everything. We can't spend every waking moment indulging our senses. Intellectual development is important, too."

"I'm wrong, then?" His smile widened. "You do know how—and when—to accept pleasure? You turn it down only when absolutely necessary?"

Lindsay's blush returned. "Possibly I've denied myself without good reason once or twice. I don't think it's done me any harm, overall."

"No doubt you wish you could really believe that."

A curt response rose to her lips but faltered on her tongue. "How can you tell what I believe?"

"Prove it, then. Come with me now. We can only resolve this in private." The hand around her waist dropped lower, his palm sliding over the curve of her rear end. Her dress rode so high that the tips of his fingers reached to the exposed part of her thigh. They slipped between her legs, skimming the edge of her panties. Meanwhile, his other hand trailed down her throat, down her front, over her breasts. "Let me tame you, pantheress."

"Yes." The word emerged from her lips spontaneously. "Yes. I do want to leave with you."

Suddenly, she spotted Caine. Without taking his eyes off them, he motioned over a server, bent, and spoke directly into her ear. Nodding, she crossed the room and approached Gabriel. He stepped away from Lindsay long enough for the server to hand him a small object. Before the transaction was complete, Caine vanished into the crowd again.

Gabriel returned to her side and held up a plastic keycard. Its face was plain black, embellished with an ornate red "P."

"Caine has reserved a room. Come."

His wintry fingers closed around hers, and Lindsay realized her hands had grown hot and sweaty. Gabriel didn't seem to mind as he led her through the crush of bodies now filling the murky space.

In no time, they'd crossed an ordinary lobby and walked to a pair of elevators Lindsay hadn't noticed before. That wasn't surprising, since no buttons lined the wall. Gabriel summoned one by inserting his keycard. When they stepped inside, Lindsay noticed that all three available floors were located underground.

Gabriel punched the center button and turned to her as the metal doors slid shut, trapping them together.

A slow shiver worked its way through Lindsay as his gaze traveled down her body. Desire burned in his eyes, but she sensed a kind of hunger, too.

"Are you going to hurt me?" she blurted. She hadn't meant to say it out loud. For some reason, Gabriel compromised her ability to separate impulse and action, just as Caine had.

"Only if you want me to."

She imagined that he sensed the heaviness between her legs, or even heard the throb of her pulse in the secret niche where her passions crouched, awaiting to unfurl at his first touch.

"No." Just in time, she remembered to stay in character. An experienced dabbler in this subculture wouldn't shy away from the prospect of a little pain introduced under certain conditions. Any hint of distaste on her part might tip Gabriel off. "I mean—that's not my thing. You sensed that earlier, and you were right."

"I'm rarely wrong. But if you change your mind, you must tell me. A little discomfort can enhance arousal."

"I'm sure it can."

"You don't understand yet. But you will."

To her relief, the elevator stopped and opened. He motioned for her to precede him into a quiet, carpeted hallway lined with doors. Gabriel paused to scan the numbers, then selected one and inserted the keycard.

The room they entered was clean to the point of sterility, its furnishings modern and the walls utterly bereft of decoration and windows, giving the impression of an underground bunker. Once again, she marveled at how seriously the patrons here took their game. Constructing an entire resort where sunlight never penetrated required serious dedication, not to mention cash.

The lack of any mirrors in the room led to thoughts about her appearance. She certainly felt grimy and disheveled after being herded, jostled, and even groped in the nightclub above.

"I'd like to freshen up," she said. Gabriel gestured toward a door in the corner. Lindsay opened it and found, to her relief, a perfectly modern bathroom complete with ornate gold spigots on the sink and a pair of complimentary robes, one crimson and one black, hanging on the wall by the glass-enclosed shower. She turned on the spray and began to peel out of her costume while the room filled with steam.

It took her a few minutes to free herself of her absurdly tight dress and its even more absurd fastenings. Finally, she stepped under a stream of scorching water and let it blast away the film of sweat and crud. Jets of heat coursed over her breasts and between her legs, heightening her anticipation for what Gabriel had planned for her.

Just outside the door, she knew, he was waiting.

Lindsay stepped out of the shower and pulled on the crimson robe. Something about its shade made her feel adventurous. At the same time, the knowledge of her hypocrisy struck her with such force that she paused, her hand on the knob.

She could try to convince herself she'd accompanied Gabriel here for the sake of her research. She could pretend that what would soon take place on the other side of the door was nothing more than an experiment, reflecting her desire for thoroughness and an inside perspective. The right jargon could make this reckless interlude sound so professional, even clinical.

The truth was that she wanted him in a way she'd never wanted any man she'd ever met over the course of her entire life. The fury of her desire both frightened and exhilarated her.

Did she really want to prove something? Normally, she would have answered "no," and felt perfectly confident in her answer. In this place, among these people, the truth seemed far more elusive.

The time had come for her to find out. Lindsay took a deep breath, steeled herself for whatever weird adventure lay ahead, and pushed open the bathroom door. A cloud of hot steam billowed out around her as she stepped forward.

Her gaze, along with her bare feet, instinctively moved to the enormous bed in the corner. Lindsay stopped to suck in her breath when she saw what awaited her there.

Gabriel lay stretched out naked on top of the covers, his fingers clasped behind his head, one leg casually crossed over the other. Only the slightest flush tinted the flat of his stomach and accented the curves of his thighs, but an aggressive, ruddy erection rose from the patch of gold hair nestled between them. The stark beauty of his pale body dazzled her, robbing her of both coherent thought and speech.

"Come closer," he ordered. With his chiseled features, pallid skin, and long flaxen mane splayed across the pillow, he resembled some haughty medieval lord, waiting for his mistress to serve him. Not for a moment did she consider doing anything else.

Lindsay complied, moving to stand at the edge of the bed. Gabriel brought his hands forward, using the left one to brace himself and sliding the right around her wrist. As he shifted his weight, his hips rolled against the blankets. His stiff cock bobbed toward her and brushed the hem of her robe, parting the front. His skin smelled fresh and cool, like newly fallen snow.

A single tug of his arm drew her onto the bed. She balanced on her knees between his open legs as he expertly relieved her of the robe. After he had tossed it to the floor, he pushed both hands up under her breasts and kneaded them with a murmur of admiration. The frostiness of his skin shocked her at first. Gradually, though, the contrast in their body temperatures seemed to lessen, as if he were drawing heat from her.

"You are soft," he whispered, bending his head and rubbing the fleshy side of her left breast over his cheek. "Warm. Your blood is filled with life."

"Y-yes," she stammered, finding her voice at last. "Of course it is. I am alive." More alive than she'd ever been before, she thought wildly.

A faint rosy blush gathered in the hollow of his throat and spread outward, filling his cheeks and chest with color. "Now you will share that life with me," he said, his voice dropping to a near growl.

His hands moved lower, too. One cupped her buttocks while the other reached between her legs. Parting her cleft with his thumb, he slid his index finger over her sensitive pearl. He smiled against her nipple when her hips bucked involuntarily and her moist folds spasmed around his fingertip.

"You're ripe and wet, like a fruit. It's been a long time since I enjoyed a fruit." His fingers probed lower, then deeper, tickling her entrance before slipping inside. Lindsay gasped with need, already teetering on the edge of orgasm. "I yearn to taste you. But not yet."

"Should we...should we get a condom?" she managed to ask. She'd left her overnight bag in the trunk of her car, wherever that had ended up. Checking the bathroom for the necessary supplies hadn't occurred to her. What was wrong with her tonight? She'd never been so careless before.

Gabriel raised his head from her breasts and laughed, this time not with sarcasm, but genuine amusement. "You know there's no need."

Lindsay scowled. She did? Yes, somehow she did. In fact, the whole idea now seemed absurd to her, though she hadn't a clue why.

All other rational thought melted when Gabriel withdrew his hand from between her legs and instead used it to coax her thighs apart. At the same time, the arm he'd wrapped around her rear end scooted her closer. Lindsay found herself straddling him, open and ready for his invasion, his rigid crown nestled in the shallows of her throbbing pussy. A single thrust from either one of them would push him inside her, something she had longed for since the moment they'd met.

Still, she hesitated, savoring instead the tantalizing rub of his stony glans against her far more fluid chasm and the delicious ache of balancing right on the precipice of utter bliss. She would be different once she joined herself to him—she knew that much, and suspected he knew it, too. Perhaps both of them were taking this last brief interlude to say goodbye to the people they were now, and would never be again.

The moment passed. Gabriel placed his hands on her hips to steady her, braced his shoulders on the bed, and pushed up the lower half of his body. He entered her in a single, forceful thrust that filled her every corner with such pleasure that the breath left her lungs and lightning flashed in her head. Everything around her went black, or rather, gold—the same brilliant gold that shone in his hair and surrounded him like an aura. She cried out as her inhibitions escaped in a single rush of breath.

The room tilted and spun, leaving her no chance to reorient herself. All her awareness converged at one particular sensation—his rapid thrusts in and out of her clasping center. Each one seemed to shatter her into a thousand sparking fragments on the downstroke, then pull her back together with every agonizing retreat. Climax hovered within reach, yet impossibly distant.

She was so caught up in the raw slap of flesh against flesh that she didn't register the sound of the door opening behind them until several seconds after the fact. Suddenly, she was aware someone else had entered the room. She managed to divide her concentration long enough to see who it was.

Caine stood a few yards away. His unreadable expression never faltered as he began to strip off his clothes.

If Gabriel noticed his friend's intrusion, he gave no indication by either slowing his movements or even looking around.

All at once, she understood. Gabriel had expected Caine all along. Each of them had a distinct role to play in her combined seduction. It was an elaborate game they had both enjoyed.

Somewhat to her own surprise, she experienced no outrage or fear at the prospect of taking on two men. Gabriel's intuition had been right on the mark. Tonight had already proved full of new experiences. Lindsay felt ready to try one more.

Leaving Caine to his preparations, she turned her attention back to Gabriel. Seconds later, the first telltale pangs of orgasm raced through her. All her concerns about Caine and whatever peculiar arrangement he had with Gabriel vanished as she came like a thunderstorm, shuddering around Gabriel's still-rigid erection, clamping her legs to his waist as if to draw him deeper inside.

Beneath their joined bodies, the bed shifted as Caine climbed on beside them. Lindsay guessed what would happen next.

But Caine didn't position his cock in front of her lips, or between her legs, or anywhere else she expected. Instead, he crouched behind her and slid his arms around her middle. His flesh, as clammy as Gabriel's had been at first, stung when he rested his full weight against her back. His swollen cock, as cool and unyielding as a marble pillar, prodded the base of her spine.

Then he leaned his head over her shoulder, swept his lips along the curve of her throat, and bit her.

Chapter 3

A silent alarm buzzed in her head as her blood flowed into Caine's mouth. Yet the sensation wasn't painful at all, but gentle, like relaxing into a deep, hot bath. Her thoughts grew muddy and her muscles went limp as his lips, now warm and full, bore down on her damp skin.

She'd been unsure, up to now, how seriously the people in this subculture took their masquerade. Now she knew. She also understood why they enjoyed it so much. The erotic charge of being stalked, seduced, and now devoured not by one, but by two gorgeous men, was enough to short-circuit her better judgment.

So she relaxed and floated.

All too soon, Caine tugged his mouth away, dabbed a brief kiss over the wound, and shifted backward. Sliding his hands under arms, Gabriel lifted her just enough to slip his cock out. Then he swapped places with his friend.

Lindsay sagged against the hard plane of Gabriel's chest, grateful for his firmness. Meanwhile, Caine gripped her legs and maneuvered her thighs over his. Still on his knees, he positioned his erection at the entrance Gabriel had abandoned. Her flesh continued to throb and pulse, her pussy eager to be filled again.

Gabriel's mouth pressed against her throat, his moist tongue licking up the blood that flowed from the wound Caine had inflicted. At the same time, Caine's cock took the place of Gabriel's, thrusting inside her as she reclined against Gabriel's body.

Caine didn't feel bigger, but his cock applied pressure in a new and equally arousing way. He seemed to stretch her wider, while

Gabriel had plunged deeper. Lindsay gasped with excitement as his plump head and shaft rubbed every nerve ending Gabriel had missed, sweeping her back to the same heights she had descended from only moments before.

His technique was different, too. He didn't piston into her rapidly or desperately, the way Gabriel had. Instead, he took her in languid, measured strokes, pausing to let her inner muscles melt around him. His fingers were busy, too, plucking at her nipples. His thumbs strummed the tiny peaks as if playing an erotic instrument.

Next, she felt another hand glide along the flat of her torso. She recognized Gabriel's fingers, longer and more delicate than Caine's, as they slid into the moist curls between her spread thighs and then moved lower. He worked his way into her engorged folds, timing his movements to match Caine's measured thrusts, and began a rhythmic massage on the tender bud hidden within.

Before long, the dual pressure on both the inside and outside of her pussy drove her over the edge. Rather than igniting in a sudden inward burst, her orgasm seeped slowly through her middle, filling her with dense, wet heat, which finally overflowed and flooded her senses. Gabriel served as her pillow as she thrashed, bucked, and dissolved into a shimmer of pure ecstasy.

Afterward, she lay back and closed her eyes. Her limbs felt heavy, and her emotions flat, as Gabriel finished feasting on her blood and shifted from beneath her. Warm blankets took the place of their skin against hers. The men stretched out beside her, one on each side, sealing her in a protective cocoon. She drifted on a half-dream, her mind seeming to separate from her body, lost in a sort of healing trance.

How much blood had they taken? She couldn't begin to guess, but she didn't feel ill. Besides, she had no way of knowing whether her weakness resulted from blood loss or from two heart-stopping orgasms in quick succession.

Caine and Gabriel began to converse over her prone, blanket-encased figure like two naked archaeologists bickering over who would take credit for the Egyptian mummy they'd just uncovered. She struggled to keep her eyes shut and her ears open, suspecting the information she gained would be worth the effort.

"I'm glad you enjoyed my gift," Caine said.

"I could have found her on my own."

"So I saved you some time. Be grateful for that, at least." Caine sighed. "You have to admit you've never tasted anything sweeter. She didn't even use the drink, you know."

"No?" Gabriel propped himself up in surprise. Lindsay assumed they were talking about the tray of odd cocktails the server had presented upon her arrival in the bar. So her suspicions had proved correct—they contained some sort of potion the so-called vampires used to enhance their experience. A date rape drug? Possible criminal activity would open up a whole new angle for her research.

"I saw her leave it on the bar."

Gabriel stroked her side through the blankets. "She's full of passion, for sure," he admitted. "In spite of your many shortcomings, Caine, I can't deny your instincts are on target…most of the time."

"I've had a lot more practice than you." Caine laughed bitterly. "Still, don't get too carried away. She isn't what she seems."

Lindsay's heart froze in her chest. Gabriel's hand fell, and his body shifted again. "What do you mean?"

"I'm not sure. But she didn't come here for the usual reasons."

"You're saying she's dangerous?"

"What does her blood tell you?"

Gabriel paused, and Lindsay felt a cold sweat prickle along the length of her spine. They could kill her, and no one would ever know what had become of her. She'd told none of her colleagues at the university where she was going. She'd left no note for Joel or anyone else. She'd wanted her research to remain secret and therefore more publishable. Perhaps she was about to pay a huge price for her recklessness.

"I tasted fear," Gabriel said after a moment. "So? Most of the new ones don't know what to expect at first. I didn't."

"Perhaps I'm mistaken. In any case, we'll figure it out. She'll stay here tomorrow. Meanwhile, I'll inform Rolando."

Lindsay tried not to let her shoulders quake as a ripple of panic shot through her. They were bringing in assistance—to help in covering up her disappearance, perhaps?

Gabriel seemed to sense her reaction. His palm returned to her hip, pressing down as if to silence her. He betrayed nothing to Caine, though.

"I'm sure she'll check out fine," he said. "She's nervous. This was her first time. And frankly, any woman with half a lick of sense ought to be frightened of you. She has good reason, whether she knows it or not."

The bed bounced as Caine stood up. "Let's not go there. I've had a good evening, and I'd like to retain that illusion, at least until I talk to Rolando."

She heard rustling sounds, probably Caine getting dressed, followed by the click of the door. Gabriel remained at her side, rocking his hand on her as if to provide comfort. He bent down until his shoulder-length hair brushed her cheek.

"I did taste deception," he whispered. "I meant what I said, though. You'd be wise to hide things from Caine. Rest now. I'll be back."

He got up and, like Caine, padded across the room to retrieve his clothes. Lindsay lay perfectly still, not even daring to breathe, her stomach and throat knotted with dread. She knew she should get up, splash water on her face, try to escape. Now that she was alone, though, the heaviness of sheer exhaustion drew itself over her. Stark black oblivion spread across her consciousness like an ink stain on pale paper. Before long, the room and its sparse furnishings faded from view.

* * * *

Lindsay had no way of telling time, but she woke certain she'd slept for quite a while. Strange, hazy memories wobbled in and out of her mind. Most of what she thought she remembered must have been a dream. She recalled hearing about a spiked drink. At the same time, she didn't think she'd actually imbibed anything.

Rising on shaky legs, she retreated to the shower and let a blast of hot water restore her. She emerged in a towel—black, of course, like most everything here—and began to look around for her clothes. She could worry about the details later, once she was back in her car and heading down the highway to safety.

Oh, no.

Either Caine or Gabriel, or more likely both of them, had taken all her possessions when they'd left the night before. That included not just her outfit, but the tiny pouch in which she'd carried her ID, some cash, and a credit card for emergencies. The robes from the bathroom were gone, too. Another memory surfaced—Caine, or maybe Gabriel, threatening to run a records check on her. They had the means to do so now. And without proper ID—or clothes—getting her car from valet parking would be tricky, at best.

"Trapped," she said aloud. Her head spun, forcing her to slump back onto the bed. She had to find a way around this. Perhaps notifying the front desk—assuming such a thing existed in this strange place—that she'd been robbed would be a good start.

Another setback followed—the room had no phone or intercom. Lurching upright, she clutched the towel around herself and went to the door. Perhaps a maid or a random guest with a kind face would walk by. When she peered out, though, she found the hallway empty except for a covered tray at her feet.

Lindsay bent down, lifted the tray, and carried it inside, struggling to keep the towel in place. Removing the lid, she discovered a warm cinnamon bun, tiny bowls of cream and sugar, and a small coffee pot exuding delicious caffeinated fumes. Though it occurred to her that these treats, like the mysterious cocktails the night before, might be drugged, she was too hungry and dizzy not to take the chance. Within moments, she had wolfed down everything.

Whoever had dropped off the tray, she figured, would return to collect it. She replaced it in the hallway and stood watch behind the door.

Soon enough, she heard the muffled rattle of the tray being picked up. Mindful of the towel's position, she leapt out into the hall.

To her astonishment, she found no one. But the tray was gone.

"This is insane," she muttered to herself. "Or at least I am."

Only seconds had elapsed. How far could the person have gone? In her towel, Lindsay set off down the hall. She kept an eye out for other trays to be collected, planning to lie in wait beside the first one she saw. No one else seemed to have left one out, though.

Suddenly, an enormous shadow rose up in front of her. She stopped so abruptly that she nearly tripped and lost her towel.

She blinked up at what turned out not to be a wall, but a perfect giant of a man. His silvery hair was buzzed around the sides, his cheeks were pale and crisscrossed with scars, and his mirrored sunglasses reflected a disturbing image of her scantily-clad self. All that kept her from screaming was his dove-gray double-breasted suit and red silk tie, complete with a diamond tiepin. Thugs didn't look so respectable, or at least she didn't think so.

"May I help you?" he asked without bothering to identify himself. His affected friendly tone frightened her more than she dared to show.

"I…uh…I was wondering if there was any kind of gift shop or something here," she improvised.

A sleek white brow rose behind the sunglasses. "I'm afraid not. What do you require?"

She clasped her hands tighter around the towel. "Isn't it obvious? I need some clothes. My overnight bag didn't make it up from my car."

The huge man bowed his head. "A careless oversight, I'm sure. I promise to see to it personally. Meanwhile, please return to your room."

It wasn't a request.

Lindsay scuttled away as fast as she could while the man reached into his jacket for a cell phone. About fifteen minutes later, she heard a knock and found her bag in the same spot as the breakfast tray. She saw no sign to indicate who had delivered it. She also realized that the man had never asked which car was hers.

Someone had gone through her bag. The contents had been jostled, the folded clothes shaken out and crammed back inside. The pages of her black spiral-bound journal were bent, as if someone had thumbed through them. That almost amused her. She'd been slow to start her research, so her idea book was virtually blank except for some random doodles where she'd tested pens before putting them in her bag. Totally innocuous.

Of course, she had plenty to write about now.

Gratefully she pulled on her jeans and a sweatshirt, then fished a pen out of her bag and turned to a blank page. She touched the tip to the paper, her mind swarming with bizarre images—the perilous road to the club, the strange people she'd seen milling about, the man on the scaffold. The memories weren't complete, and few of them made sense, but further research would help sort that out. For now, a series of brief descriptions would do to get her started.

A strange thing happened when she touched the pen to the paper, though. Her fingers stiffened, her mind went blank, and she found herself utterly unable to make even the slightest mark.

"I'm overtired," she guessed, speaking out loud to herself, as she often did when trying to work out a puzzling situation. "Need to rest." Maybe she was dreaming now. She couldn't be sure.

She crawled back on the bed, closed her eyes, and tried to organize her thoughts. As her mind moved in and out of sleep, certain images became clearer, while others got hazier. She now remembered the naked man in the club, and the women swarming around him with the knives. He enjoyed what they did to him, Caine had explained. Then, later, Caine had shown her firsthand what happened when the participants got deeper into the game. Gabriel had taken part, too. They'd pretended to bite her, to drink her blood. They'd bantered as though they were vampires.

And they'd given her the best sex she'd ever had.

She sat up, her body tingling all over with pleasures she could distinctly recall now. Her notebook lay at the foot of the bed, where she'd tossed it earlier when exhaustion overcame her. Leaning down, she snatched it up and shook the pen from the folds of the bedspread.

Again she started to capture in words some of the bizarre pictures trapped in her head. And again, the only result was a series of haphazard scribbles.

Startled, she set the pen down and flexed her hand, then tried again. Nothing.

"My fault, I'm afraid," Caine's voice broke in on her thoughts. He'd appeared out of nowhere, leaning against the closed door. She hadn't heard it open or shut. "My bite has bound us together. It will be impossible for you to describe what's passed between us to any third party, including an inanimate object like a notebook or a tape recorder."

"You're controlling my thoughts?" She hadn't meant to sound incredulous, but the very idea was so preposterous that she forgot the role she had to play and lapsed into her usual, overly rational self.

"Not exactly controlling them." Crossing his arms, he scrutinized her intently, tempting her to avert her eyes. She forced herself not to. Of course, that wasn't a difficult task. He looked delicious, having changed into a sleek black suit that framed his tall, lean figure to perfection—even if the shirt underneath, black as well, accentuated the pallor of his skin. Why was every good-looking guy she met totally nuts? "We're connected now, at a level no human can even imagine. I'm part of your subconscious. Our connection makes it impossible for you to betray me or Gabriel. Not that I'm assuming betrayal was your intention."

"I don't want to betray you," she said.

He scowled, his fingers tightening on his sleeves, but she didn't flinch. "Are you a reporter?" he demanded, glancing down at the blank page in front of her.

"No."

"Some sort of a writer, then. You want to record what you've experienced here. That's why the bond kicked in. If you'd been writing a grocery list, your hand wouldn't have faltered."

"I'm keeping a diary. I write for my own pleasure. To make sense of my experiences."

"Keeping journals was all the rage when I was a young man," he admitted. "I didn't think humans did that anymore."

"Plenty of humans keep journals. Go to any bookstore and you'll see rows and rows of blank ones. Someone must be writing in them."

Abandoning that topic, Caine moved onto a new line of questioning. "I should have asked you this last night. How did you find out about Purgatory?"

Lindsay shrugged, forcing herself to appear nonchalant and hoping he didn't also consider himself an expert at reading body language as well as minds. "I grew up in a town called Darkisle, just a couple of hours down the coast. It's a gloomy town...and boring. Some of the kids I went to high school with got on a Goth kick. A few claimed to have been here. The rumors got me curious about this place, but I never believed it existed. Recently I uncovered the location through...sources. I decided to check it out for myself. And here I am. Blank journal and all."

"I'm inclined to believe that, since Purgatory is impossible to find without specific directions. Strong penalties exist for giving out the location indiscriminately. Whoever gave you the information trusted you."

"True. But I can't say any more than that."

Caine unfolded his arms. "We have to protect ourselves, Lindsay Tanner. You understand, I'm sure."

"If it's any consolation, it took me hours and hours to find my way here. I got lost plenty of times, and my GPS quit working."

"That was no accident. Rolando, the owner, has installed transmitters to block and scramble such devices for miles around."

Rolando—she'd heard that name before. This time she did suffer a physical twinge. Caine had mentioned Rolando in connection with checking her out, she remembered, and possibly in connection with more sinister activities.

"Where...where is Gabriel?" she asked. She couldn't bring herself to believe Caine had come here alone to hurt her...or was she deluding herself about his intentions?

"He'll be along. He's much slower at getting ready than I am."

"Getting ready for what?"

Caine's white teeth glistened. "For you, of course. We want to take you back upstairs to the club."

"The club?" she repeated, feeling as though she were failing to grasp something obvious. "It can't be open at this hour. It's still morning...isn't it?"

"No, my dear. It's well past six in the evening. The club will open as soon as the sun goes down...a little less than an hour, by my calculations."

Lindsay's eyes widened. Her head felt light again. In this windowless, underground room, she realized, time and place had no real meaning. The outside world could have ceased to exist, and she would never know. Likewise, Caine could bring her news of its destruction, and she would have no way of confirming his story.

"I've been asleep all day?" she marveled.

"The rest did you good. Gabriel and I both took your blood last night. We went too far for your first time. However, we couldn't help ourselves. I hope you were not emotionally overwhelmed. Physically, you seem unharmed."

"I'm fine. I'm just...a little disoriented." She shook her head, then lowered it into her hands and rubbed her temples in an attempt to focus her thoughts. "So I really was with both of you last night. Funny...it almost seems like a dream."

To her surprise, the voice that answered wasn't Caine's. It was Gabriel's.

"If it was a dream," he said quietly, "would you like to have the same one again?"

Her answer came without a moment's hesitation.

"Yes...oh, yes."

Chapter 4

The two men—or vampires—required no further enticement.

Caine stepped forward first. Sliding his arms around her waist, he gripped the hem of her sweatshirt and peeled it over her head. He discarded it along with his jacket and returned his attentions to her freed breasts. His palms traced the delicate arc of her ribs while his fingers stretched upward to caress her nipples.

Meanwhile, Gabriel moved to stand behind her. Resting his chin on her bare shoulder, he reached around to undo the top button of her jeans. Her zipper gave way with a drawn-out whisper of anticipation.

She gasped as his cool palms skimmed the curve of her hips and then dropped lower, pushing her pants down. Shocks of arousal rushed through her when he bared her thighs and ran his hands over their soft planes with obvious appreciation. His thumbs pressed deeper, tracing a path to the more intimate juncture between. Soon his index fingers joined them, drawing out her nectar in gentle, measured strokes.

The combination of four hands on her body made her dizzy. Her senses blurred even further when Gabriel dragged his lips across her shoulder. She shivered, as if someone had sprinkled a handful of snowflakes over her hot skin. Yet she was the one who melted into his touch.

Caine paused. "We can't feed on her tonight," he said, addressing his comments to Gabriel. "We would leave her too weak."

"I know." Gabriel's fingers moved inside her, making her writhe in a surge of pleasure. "Give me a little credit."

"A tiny sampling, though, would be in order." Through half-closed eyes, Lindsay saw Caine smile. "She's hard to resist."

"Agreed."

They moved her over to the bed and joined her, clothed, on top of the covers. After they'd settled her on the pillows, Gabriel knelt between her legs and replaced his fingers with his tongue.

His mouth was surprisingly tender, and skilled beyond reason, against her intimate folds. He licked at her swollen flesh, his upper lip pressed at her engorged bud. Soon, she trembled at the slight graze of his teeth. Was he planning to take her blood from there?

Of course not, she reminded herself, struggling to rein in her imagination. Gabriel wasn't a vampire, and neither was Caine. Real vampires didn't exist. Once they left this club, she was certain, they became ordinary men with ordinary jobs, their fantasies under wraps until they ventured out into the safe zone of their subculture again. Like most everything else she studied in her field, it all came down to constructing one's sexual identity. Theirs was kinkier than some people's and a lot tamer than others'.

At least…that had been her theory until now. The coolness of their touch and the extreme grace and precision with which they moved made her wonder if something more might be going on. By the time the three were entwined on the bed, though, she no longer cared what they were or might have been. She only knew she couldn't get enough of them.

While Gabriel continued to administer the most intimate of kisses, Caine cupped her breasts in his hands, fingers stroking her nubs to the utmost sensitivity. His mouth soon settled on the curve of her ear and moved lower, back to the same spot he'd bitten the night before. Slowly, he laved the area with his tongue. His cool saliva had a soothing effect on her skin, like a potent balm or even a topical anesthetic. Then he paused again, waiting for something—what?

She got her answer when Gabriel's mouth coaxed her to the first shudders of climax. All of a sudden, shards of pleasure splintered through her body like twin bolts of wet lightning—one from above, one from below her heaving middle. Every muscle, inside and out, clenched up tight enough to lift her lower body from the bed. Moaning, bucking, she arched her back and lost herself in the most delicious abandon she could ever imagine, or even imagine imagining.

No sooner had that sensation begun to wear off than an entirely new one surged through her. Lindsay had heard about women who could climax in their nipples, but she'd always written it off as a figment of their imaginations. A few caresses later, she was experiencing it herself. The thrill hummed through her, burning a line straight from her tits to her pussy.

At the precise moment she hit her second peak, Caine bit down, reopening the wound on her neck. Gabriel's teeth entered her skin, too—in the sensitive place just beside her pubic hairline. Contrary to all her expectations, he really was biting her there, and, equally surprising, it felt wonderful.

Lindsay perceived the slightest sting, superseded by the beautiful sensation of rising, falling, coasting, and losing herself. When Caine lifted his head, she was barely aware of it because Gabriel was still busy between her throbbing legs.

Through a haze of bliss, she saw Caine reach out across her and grasp a handful of Gabriel's glossy hair. Gabriel snarled as his lips were forced away from her skin.

"Enough," Caine said sternly. "Remember what we talked about before. I won't allow you to hurt her because you can't control yourself."

"I can control myself just fine," Gabriel snarled. But he did back away from her, much to her disappointment.

The three of them stretched out together, her bare legs entwined in their clothed ones. Caine slung his left arm over her waist and nestled his face into the gap between her ear and the base of her skull. Gabriel rested his head against her breasts, his fingers spread over her midriff.

Lindsay lay in a state of complete contentment, her nerves still buzzing and her blood thundering in her veins. Sleep beckoned, but at the same time she had never been so aware of her surroundings...especially the two men surrounding her.

Gabriel's eyes widened when she wrenched his chunky belt buckle open. She groped inside, wrapping her fingers around his thick erection. Her other hand reached behind to toy with Caine's fly. He, too, was plump with desire for her, his fleshy bulge straining at the fabric.

His deep sigh was edged with pain as he pushed her hand away. "We need to get up. Gabriel and I have plans for you this evening."

Lindsay was too besotted with their company even to question whether those plans should fill her with anticipation or dread. "Can't we stay here a while?" she coaxed. Her thumb skidded over the tender tip of Gabriel's crown, causing him to twitch and groan.

"No." Caine's voice remained stern. "In the state we're both in, it would be reckless—not to mention dangerous for you. Gabriel and I will take our nourishment in the club. Perhaps later, when the urge to feed on you isn't as strong, we can venture in another direction."

He extracted his limbs from hers in a single, determined movement, and crossed the room in three quick strides. Lindsay suppressed her amusement as he loosened his belt, stuffed his dark shirt back into his pants, and pulled his jacket back on.

"Caine's right." Gabriel brushed his lips across her nipple before rolling away and climbing to his feet as well. "We're asking for trouble if we stay here."

Lindsay looked up at him with a fresh throb of desire. His pants still hung open, affording her just a glimpse of the temptation within. She accepted his proffered hand and allowed him to pull her up, gratified to see the mound shift and swell in response to her touch.

Still holding her wrist, Gabriel swept a sheet off the bed and thrust it toward her. "Cover yourself. I can't be responsible for my actions otherwise."

Lindsay wrapped the sheet around herself. "You guys take this vampire thing pretty seriously," she said in an attempt to lighten the mood. Neither of their faces showed the slightest flicker of amusement.

Caine cleared his throat. "I suggest you take it seriously, too, if you value your own well-being." He hadn't spoken the words as a threat, but as simple fact.

"I get the sense you don't quite understand what you've stumbled into here," Gabriel said, zipping his pants. "You don't know as much about vampire culture as you pretend."

"Well...I've never denied that this is all new to me," Lindsay said, determined not to stammer. "But I came here to find out more."

Caine moved to stand beside Gabriel. "If you want to learn about vampires, Gabriel and I can teach you."

"Of course I do." She didn't need to pretend this time. What researcher into a closed underground culture wouldn't jump at the chance to be shown around by two insiders? A few more hours with them would yield enough information to fill half the pages of her doctoral thesis, if not the entire thing. In fact, her mind was already racing past academic accomplishments and onto more lucrative paths—book contracts, magazine exposés, afternoon talk shows. People made pots of money by analyzing the sexual kinks of strangers. Maybe she could do the same.

"All right, then." Caine nodded. "Here's the catch—you can't reveal anything you see or hear to another living soul." At last, his lips curled into something resembling a smile. "The bond, remember?"

"I understand."

This time, her voice did falter a bit. Was it unethical for her to agree to keep their secrets while planning to build a career on broadcasting them?

Then again, she wasn't promising anything. She'd simply indicated that she understood what Caine was saying. That little semantic dodge would have to salve her conscience for now.

Or was he referring to this bizarre mind-control thing he seemed to believe in? That, at least, she wasn't worried about at all. What she'd experienced earlier was no doubt run-of-the-mill writer's block—something she'd dealt with plenty of times throughout her academic career. She'd overcome it before and would do so again.

"Glad to hear it." Caine bent and picked up her overnight bag. "Let's get you dressed, then. Things should just be getting underway upstairs."

He tossed her the bag, and with a nod, she slipped into the bathroom and turned the shower up full force. Grateful to be away from their scrutiny, she took her time under the water. Though she heard the door open and the sink run a couple of times, neither of the men disturbed her.

She emerged in a tight red dress, the shoulders exposed, the hem just long enough to be decent. At least she'd had the foresight to include an extra "party" outfit, which she'd rolled up and stowed in the bottom of her bag. Her boots had been stuffed into the bag as well. Though she hadn't put them there, she was too grateful to have them back to dwell on the efficiency of Purgatory's spies.

Each of them reached out to take one of her hands. Lindsay's pulse quickened at the sensuality of their touch.

Gabriel's eyes widened a little, the way her own did when some succulent chocolate dessert was set down in front of her, while Caine swiped his tongue over his swelling lips.

"Beautiful," Gabriel whispered. "I wish—"

"Not now," Caine snapped, cutting him off. "Let's go."

They stepped into the hall together, one man on either side of her, each holding one of her hands. No one else appeared on their brief journey to the elevator, and no one tried to prevent her from leaving her room, or the floor, this time.

Belatedly, she wondered if their firm grip on her might not be the result of affection, but an attempt to block an escape. Pushing her misgivings aside, she focused instead on how liberated and bold she felt, striding through the hotel with her two handsome lovers. If anyone in the club found their arrangement odd, no one they passed gave any indication.

They entered the same barroom she'd walked into as a complete newbie less than twenty-four hours earlier. She could hardly fathom how much had changed in such a short span of time—and how much she had changed.

The people in the bar seemed to notice, too. The night before, she'd felt more or less ignored. Tonight, more than a few of them, both men and women, looked up at her with blatant interest.

The same server approached her, too, holding the same tray of colorful drinks. She stepped between Lindsay and the two men under the pretext of offering her one.

"You did all right, I see," the server confided, leaning close. "I sure admire you, going for double. I don't think I could hold out long enough."

She reached out with her free hand and pushed Lindsay's hair aside, exposing the very spot where Caine had earlier licked her wound closed.

"Nice job," the woman commented. "Those two know what they're doing—I could see that right away. Not like some of the other brutes in here. They think it's still the thirteenth century. No technique at all."

"I think I did meet the guy you mean," Lindsay said, trying not to look startled. "Luckily, it was a brief encounter."

"Yeah, Rolando's thinking of eighty-sixing that creep. Too bad, because he has nowhere else to go, but I say we have to draw the line somewhere. He tried to grope me the other day, too. I was thinking of bringing in some garlic spray."

"Would that work?" Lindsay asked, incredulous.

"As long as he thinks it does." The woman winked. "The vampires were as superstitious as the humans in his world. We can use that to our advantage with his type."

When the woman handed her a drink—the same color she'd selected the night before—and moved on, Lindsay touched her own neck and frowned. Only the slightest bump remained in the spot Caine had sunk his teeth into. She remembered the rush of pleasure mixed with pain as his lips closed over the breach in her flesh and coaxed the sweet fluid from her veins.

At least, she thought she remembered it. Now she wondered if, in the heat of the moment, she had imagined some of the details. After all, neck wounds didn't heal that fast.

The alternative explanation wasn't an option.

Gabriel stood at her side again. He stared down at the drink she held.

"Is this safe?" she asked, holding it up for his scrutiny.

"Of course. Why wouldn't it be?"

"Well, you know, I've heard about clubs spiking their drinks to make people more…vulnerable."

"Nothing illegal goes on here." Gabriel sounded a bit impatient.

"Relax," Caine said, sliding in beside her as well. "We're supposed to explain things to her, not get defensive. Let's start with the basics." He pointed to a tall, steel-faced man walking around the bar and nearby tables as if on an inspection tour. "That's Rolando, the owner of Purgatory. He's old—about four hundred, give or take, but not the oldest specimen you'll meet here."

Lindsay scowled. "Four hundred?"

"Years, of course. Surely you know vampires don't age. That was one thing the movies did get right."

"I…see."

"Rolando's mate is human. She provides him with blood. Therefore, he no longer hunts—here or anywhere else. He gets everything he needs to survive in the bedroom, or wherever the urge takes him." Caine's smile tilted. "Rolando is a bit of a wild one."

"That doesn't hurt her?"

"So far, he's managed to take just what he needs. They've been together quite a while."

"Both of us feasted on you, and you're not hurt," Gabriel pointed out.

"Many humans find feeding a vampire pleasurable," Caine said. "Some even become addicted. It's like a sex act, but far, far more intimate. Done properly, it's as safe as donating a pint or two to the local Red Cross wagon."

"Some of which are run by vampires, by the way," Gabriel said. "If you ever see a blood drive at night, you should scrutinize the volunteers."

Caine laughed. "They never seem to miss a few bags. Creative paperwork."

"So all of these people are…vampires?" Lindsay looked around, bewildered. Aside from a few odd costumes, they looked like the patrons in any urban bar that catered to eccentric tastes.

Gabriel shook his head. "Donors, mostly. The vampires don't waste their time up here. This area is for the dabblers."

Lindsay remembered the cheers of encouragement when she'd so naively charged into the back room the night before. No question about it, she could have gotten herself into real trouble here. Thank goodness she'd run into Caine and Gabriel when she had.

"Come on." Caine motioned for her to follow. "Let's go where the real action is. Gabriel and I need to feed."

Gabriel fell into place behind her, and the three of them moved through the outer bar into the space where she had seen the man tied to the scaffolding. This area, too, was filling fast, and she endured a round of lecherous looks as Caine led the way to a thick metal door she hadn't noticed the night before.

It opened into a shadowed passageway that ended in three stone steps. The atmosphere below was murky, the only illumination provided by small round portals recessed into the brick walls. Lindsay expected to see candles or sconces, but she supposed such materials would pose a fire hazard.

Ahead of them, silhouetted figures ambled through the gloom. The low rumble of conversation replaced the throb of techno music. Some of the voices spoke in languages Lindsay didn't understand or even recognize.

It's all a game, she reminded herself. The people here were simply that—people, even if their delusions did have the potential to make them dangerous. And she'd already reconciled herself to that risk.

When her eyes adjusted to the near-darkness, she realized that the space they had entered resembled not a dungeon, after all, but the dingy opium dens she'd seen depicted in books about earlier centuries. Antique-looking tables and chairs, all mismatched, were pushed against the walls. Sullen men and women, both alone and in groups, lounged in them. Some drank from the same type of metal goblet she'd seen Gabriel holding when they'd first met.

Once again, several pairs of eyes focused on her as she accompanied her two escorts to one of the tables. Lindsay clutched her ridiculous pink cocktail to her chest, grateful she'd brought it with her. Hopefully no one would ask her to sample any of the strange concoctions they probably served down here.

An odd, musty smell tickled her nose. Rising above the heady mixture came another sharp, metallic scent...was it human blood?

For the first time, she experienced a genuine stab of fear. Clearly, this was an area the club restricted to its most privileged members. Considering the eccentric pastimes the mainstream patrons indulged in, she could only imagine what went on down here.

This vampire game was far more complex than she'd realized.

Chapter 5

"Does this room frighten you?" Caine asked as they moved to a table at the back of the room.

"No."

Her obvious lie prompted a laugh. "It should. This space is the ultimate refuge for those who share our condition. The walls are constructed to block even the hint of sunlight. Here, we can stay awake all day, if the urge strikes us, though there are compartments in the stone for patrons who wish to rest."

"Or invite a donor to a more private spot," Gabriel added.

"True. Though plenty like to be watched, or envied, in the act of satiation."

Lindsay shuddered, but decided they were trying to impress her. Playing along was her best option.

When they had taken their seats, a new serving woman—this one dressed in a brief, Egyptian-style tunic and a few silver chains looped over her body—deposited goblets in front of Caine and Gabriel. Lindsay made sure to place her fruit drink prominently in front of her. To her relief, the woman ignored her.

Somewhat to Lindsay's surprise, neither man proposed a toast or even glanced at what was in their goblets. Instead, they picked them up in unison and drank, quickly and greedily. Caine's face contorted into a desperate expression, while Gabriel looked as though he were easing some terrible inner pain.

Lindsay watched, astonished at the physiological changes the refreshments had on them both. Their pale, hollow cheeks plumped and reddened, their lips grew fuller and moister, and their attitudes grew more relaxed. No alcoholic drinks she'd ever heard of, however strong, caused such an immediate and transformative effect.

Noticing her stare, Caine set down his cup with a thump. "You should be safe for a while now, my dear. That took the edge off."

"Aged to perfection," Gabriel agreed.

"What...what was that?" Lindsay forced herself to ask.

Caine's eyes hardened. "What do you think?" He relented a bit when she flinched. "But don't worry. It was offered voluntarily and sanitized by experts. You'll find no discarded heaps of corpses in the back room. Whoever gave us this gift is alive and happy, and most likely dancing the night away upstairs."

A queasy rush made her stomach flutter. She snatched her hand away from the stem of her own glass.

"What's...what's in mine, then?"

"A combination of sugar, food coloring, and rum," Gabriel said. "Sweetens the blood. Harmless to you. It won't even get you drunk, unless you knock back ten glasses."

Caine nodded. "Your blood is perfect without any additives. I prefer a more natural flavor, myself. Same goes for every part of a woman." He punctuated his declaration with a lecherous wink.

Lindsay blushed, partly from embarrassment and partly from apprehension. Before she thought of a suitable response, though, a loud disturbance erupted at a nearby table. The three of them turned, along with everyone else in the room, to another table where a man and his three companions were arguing. At least Lindsay recognized French this time, though the dialect sounded like nothing she'd heard in the language lab at college. She couldn't quite decipher what they were saying, though the tone suggested the majority of the diatribe consisted of curse words.

The man who had been shouting the loudest leaped to his feet and slammed both hands on the table, making his companions' goblets jump. Then he whirled and swept from the room, his long coattails flapping behind him. As he passed their table, Lindsay's mouth opened in surprise. The man was dressed like a member of Louis XVI's court, complete with a lacy cravat and a fluffy powdered wig. In fact, most everyone around them wore odd costumes, some strange mixtures of antiquated and modern fashions. Odd, raucous laughter followed the angry man as he marched up the stone steps and vanished from sight.

"They like to pretend they're back in their own time," Caine explained. "Me, I'll take the modern world any time. The clothes are more comfortable and people smell a lot better."

He looked up suddenly, and she realized that not everyone at the table had remained seated after the quarrel. The man who stood glowering down at them had a cleaner and more intact shirt on this time, and his grizzled hair was pulled back in a haphazard ponytail. His fierce eyes and mottled skin looked all too familiar, though. In the poor lighting, she hadn't recognized her attacker from the night before.

He mumbled something unintelligible to Caine, then reached into his pocket and threw a few antique coins into the center of the table. Without hesitation, Caine grunted and swept the money back toward him.

"He's offering to buy you," Gabriel whispered to Lindsay. "Poor sod doesn't have a clue."

Before Gabriel finished speaking, the man's arm lashed out, his gnarled fingers reaching for Lindsay's throat. A horrible, feral growl twisted his gray lips.

"Whoa!" Gabriel leapt to his feet and planted himself between Lindsay and the intruder. "Back off. Now."

"He won't listen," Caine said, standing as well. His hand, warm and lightning-fast, landed on her shoulder. "Get under the table," he ordered as he pushed her down. Other patrons crowded around, jostling each other in anticipation of a show.

Crouching so she could watch them over the top of the table, Lindsay saw the gray-haired man reach down and pull an ornate curved dagger from his boot. Before Gabriel was able to stop him, he sprang forward with a roar and slashed the knife straight across Caine's chest.

Lindsay screamed as Caine staggered back, both hands pressed to the injured site. He dropped them a moment later to reveal a vicious cut across his shirt and the front of his jacket.

But he wasn't bleeding. How had the blade failed to break the skin? Maybe in the same way Caine's filed teeth had failed to leave a mark on hers?

She had little time to ponder the matter as Gabriel, tense for battle, stepped beside Caine. They had attracted a crowd of about twenty men and women now. The crowd's eyes glowed with anticipation. Some opened their mouths as if to shout encouragement to the combatants…or take a bite out of one of them. Even in the near-darkness, Lindsay saw the glint of pearly fangs and hunger-moistened lips.

Furious, and still wielding the dagger, the man bellowed and flung himself at Caine and Gabriel. A plan, no doubt fueled by her own pumping adrenaline, provided instant inspiration. This time, Lindsay did duck all the way under the table and crawled far enough forward to grab one of the man's booted ankles.

He hadn't expected it, and the gesture pulled him off balance just as his feet left the floor. Howling in anger, he toppled over like a marble statue and took the entire table down with him. The empty goblets rolled onto him and bounced off his back, while the colorful cocktail she'd left untouched anointed his grubby hair with a cheerful splash of pink. Lifting his wet hands in the air, he wailed as if he'd been doused with something toxic.

By then a cadre of bouncers, among them the man Caine had earlier identified as Rolando, hurried over to separate them. To Lindsay's relief, the crowd now turned its attention to Rolando's attempt to calm the miscreant.

"Enough!" Rolando barked. "You're not hurt. Time you learned to shower, anyway."

His presence had an immediate calming effect on everyone in the room except their attacker, who rolled back onto his knees as if preparing for another round. "I already told you, we don't behave like animals around here. Times have changed," Rolando explained while members of his staff held the struggling man in place. "Women aren't property any more. Even those like us have to abide by the law."

Caine pulled Lindsay to her feet. "Time to get out of here, don't you think?"

Her weary gaze telegraphed her agreement.

No one interfered as the three of them slipped back up the steps and returned to the less perilous environment above.

Lindsay assumed the three of them would resume their evening's entertainment in another part of the club, but instead Caine led them to the elevators.

The whole way, he cursed about his ruined outfit. "First time I wore this, too. Disgusting barbarian. I have a score to settle with whoever released him from that tomb."

His attitude stunned her. "You were slashed with a knife and you're worried about your clothes? You could have been killed!"

"With that puny dagger? The blade wasn't even sharp." Caine grinned. "What good is immortality if you can't use it to intimidate your enemies…or impress your dates?"

Lindsay had no answer. She glanced at the elevators. Neither Caine nor Gabriel had pushed the button to summon one. "Um…where are we going?" Up to the room for more sex? She hoped so, though she couldn't quite bring herself to voice her desire.

"Actually, I think we ought to make our exit. I'm tired of this place, though it's served its purpose. We own a house about an hour from here. Or should I say, Gabriel owns it. He allows me to stay as his guest now and again."

Lindsay stared, trying not to let her surprise and disappointment show. Of course she'd known her interlude with them couldn't go on forever. She'd planned to return to Boston after a night or two, with a notebook full of observations she could start translating into the requisitely dry academic prose. Physical pleasure had never factored into the equation, much less a continuing liaison with her research subjects.

And yet...against all logic, not to mention her better judgment, she didn't want her time with them to end.

After an agonizing moment, Caine added, "You're welcome to come with us. I don't think Gabriel would object."

"Certainly not," Gabriel said. "Consider yourself invited."

Lindsay exhaled heavily. Did she dare to do this? Such rash behavior went against everything she was or had ever been.

"I'm...I'm not sure."

Caine scoffed. "You have exactly fifteen minutes to decide. By then we'll need to be on the road if we're to get home before sunup."

He walked away without inviting them to follow.

"You will come with us?" Gabriel prodded. "I promise to make you comfortable and safe. And you'll be free to leave at any time...though I hope you won't."

As she always did when faced with a dilemma, she decided to focus on practical matters first. "Uh...Where would I check out?" she asked.

"Don't worry," Gabriel reassured her. "Caine's had a standing account here for years. He'll take care of everything. He'll have your things packed up and brought to your car, too."

"Oh." Lindsay felt a little foolish when she realized she'd forgotten about her car. She felt a little more secure knowing she would have some means of transportation at their house. That way, she could take off if things got uncomfortable...assuming Gabriel was telling the truth about letting her go.

She swallowed. If she said no, these two men would fade from her life forever. Was she reckless to place that concern above her own safety?

Hadn't that always been her problem, though—an inability to open herself up to possibilities, to let the good slip away with the bad? A judgmental voice echoed deep in her memory. *That's what's wrong with you, Lindsay. You won't take chances. You're boring. And, frankly, you bore me. Good-bye.*

"Yes." She met his expectant gaze with a confidence she forced herself to feel. "I'll come with you."

"You're sure?"

"I'm sure."

Gabriel's face relaxed into a smile that made her insides clench with desire. "All right, then." He took out a cell phone and spoke briefly to someone she assumed was Caine. "It's a go. See you there." He snapped the phone shut and looked up at her happily. "Caine will drive your car. You and I will go in mine. Don't worry. He's a good driver."

She was about to ask why she couldn't take her own vehicle when a possible explanation dawned on her. Maybe they didn't want her to be able to find their house on her own once she left.

Assuming they ever allowed her to leave.

It wasn't too late to change her mind. She could walk away now, make a run for the parking lot, disappear into the night. They would never find her. She doubted they would even look.

"Gabriel—"

He slid an arm around her waist and hugged her to him.

"I'm glad you're coming," he said. "We fit together. Don't you feel the same?"

The excuse she was about to make withered on her parted lips.

"Yes," she said. "I do."

Gabriel led her back through the lobby and out to the circular driveway. The same gaunt valet spotted them and shuffled off to find

Gabriel's car. Lindsay stared at him a bit longer this time than she had when she'd first arrived. Given everything she'd seen in the club, his peculiar appearance and sunken eyes no longer seemed the result of poor genetics or deliberate costuming. His gait, too, suggested someone with unnaturally poor muscle coordination—or some sort of revivified ghoul from a black-and-white horror movie.

Impossible, she reminded herself. This was all an illusion, designed by people who had elevated a leisure activity to an art form.

When the car arrived—a sleek, expensive-looking model that glowed flame orange under the street lamp—Gabriel moved around to the passenger side and opened the door for her. She slid into the buttery leather seat and allowed him to buckle the seatbelt around her.

"I promised to keep you safe," he joked. The attempt to ease her worries proved only partially successful. Every moment, she became more painfully aware of her foolhardiness in putting herself under their control like this. But when she remembered the gentleness of Gabriel's hands on her skin, and the raw power of his cock inside her, and the uninhibited way she came with him—with both of them—she wanted to trust them. The connection Caine had spoken of, whatever it consisted of, went three ways. She knew that as instinctively as she knew her own name.

Soon they were speeding down an unlit, unpaved road surrounded on all sides by impenetrable wilderness. She didn't recognize anything around them, nor did Gabriel's headlights illuminate a single road sign. Her own car failed to appear, either in front of them or in the rear-view mirror.

They didn't speak for several long, tense minutes.

"Gabriel," she finally ventured, "I need to ask you something. It's been on my mind since last night."

He shrugged without taking his eyes off the road. "Shoot."

"You and Caine. The whole dynamic between you. The way he just showed up when we were together. Do the two of you...uh...I mean, are you and he...?"

He let her flounder a bit, enjoying her discomfort, before laughing. "Gay? No. He and I are not physically interested in one another. We do share a bond, but one that goes much deeper than sex. You see, he made me a vampire. That ties us together for eternity. Sharing our bodies would almost be anticlimactic—so to speak."

Lindsay sat up with interest. This was just the sort of information she needed for her research. "Um…how did he do that, exactly?"

"How do you think? He drained me of blood and left me to die. Probably watched the whole time, enjoying every minute. Luckily, I don't remember too much. It happened a long time ago."

"Oh." She didn't know how to respond to the sudden bitterness that crept into his voice. "Well, then, do you and Caine always share women? Or was there something special about me?"

"You know very well there's something special about you." To her relief, he seemed to recover some of his former good spirits. "But no, not too often. We had a falling out once. That soured things for a while. With you, though…it seemed time to take a chance again."

"What was the argument about?"

His jaw tensed. "You don't want to hear about that, any more than I want to discuss it. It has nothing to do with you, or with us."

"I'm sorry. I didn't mean to open old wounds."

"That's an interesting choice of words. But don't be sorry. Just let it go."

"All right." At least for now, she added under her breath.

True to his word, about an hour later Gabriel pulled into a driveway she would never have seen, the dirt thread tucked between a tangle of low-hanging tree branches and coiled knots of bittersweet. The headlights swept the front of an old-fashioned two-story stone house. Whatever charm it once held had fallen victim to large splotches of moss and dark, parasitic vines that clung to the eaves and windows.

Inexplicably, her car sat in the driveway. That meant Caine was inside.

When Gabriel cut the engine, inky darkness swallowed the house and the surrounding woodland. The faded moon provided just enough light to make out what lay directly beside and in front of them.

Though Lindsay couldn't see the ocean, she smelled the crisp, salty wind as soon as she stepped onto the gravel. They were near the sea, obviously, but beyond that she felt displaced, as though she'd lost all sense of direction during the trip.

"Your house is interesting," she said, unable to think of a more flattering word, as Gabriel came to stand beside her. 'Beautiful' would have stood out as a lie, though she sensed it had the potential to become an attractive property. The brief glance she'd enjoyed suggested that the place had fallen into disrepair from deliberate neglect. Scraping the moss and trimming the overgrown branches, scouring the windows, and landscaping the yard would have improved it considerably.

"Caine bought it for me out of guilt, you know."

So that was it. Displaced aggression. By neglecting the house, he let Caine know he was neglecting him.

"Guilt for what?" Years of training in psychology told her to feign naïveté. People were far more likely to open up that way.

"Isn't it obvious? For taking my life. For turning me into a vampire." Gabriel frowned and gazed in the direction of the house as if viewing it for the first time, though she couldn't figure out how he could see anything. She certainly couldn't. "I know what you're going to say. After one hundred and fifty years, I should let it go. But tell me this—would you ever truly forgive a man who killed you, even if you continued to exist?"

The question left her confused. "I–I don't know," she finally stammered. "Obviously, I've never thought about it. Anyhow, that wasn't what I was going to say."

"Oh? Perhaps my mind-reading abilities have failed me." He smiled at her startled expression. "Don't worry. Vampires can't read minds. That's another lurid Hollywood fable. We are sensitive to other people's expressions, tiny tics in their voices, things like that. No different than what your average FBI profiler does. Our heightened senses just make us far more effective at it. In fact, the FBI employs a number of vampires. They're the best. I'll bet you never knew that."

"I didn't." She chewed her lip. The mention of the FBI unsettled her. Much like an undercover agent, she'd sneaked into their lives to do her own investigation, and found out far more than she could process, at least right away.

No doubt undercover cops went through these same mental contortions—not to mention the guilt and uncertainty. In weak moments, some probably slept with their suspects, as she had.

And some of them didn't come home from their assignments, either. She thought of her cousin's warning. Would any smart cop be here, now, in the middle of nowhere, with two guys pretending to be vampires? Doubtful.

Still, her car was here. They hadn't lied about that.

"Come on," he said, taking her hand. "Caine will be waiting."

Chapter 6

His fingers curled around hers protectively. Together, they walked up the rock- and weed-strewn path and stepped inside the front door. The latch stood open for them, and the lights were already on.

To call the furnishings sparse would have been an understatement. A jumble of chairs and small tables lay strewn around in no particular order, and a few age-darkened paintings of indifferent subjects like landscapes and still-life arrangements hung crookedly on the walls. Everything looked clean enough, but the air tasted frigid and sterile.

"Well, what do you think, Lindsay?" Gabriel asked.

"It's chilly," she said, hugging her arms together.

"Yes, I expected you to find the temperature uncomfortable. Caine and I are cold-blooded now, physiologically speaking, and fires hold little appeal for us, for a number of reasons. But don't worry. We have all the modern facilities—they just haven't been used in a long time. Come, I'll show you to the guest room."

He led her up a set of stairs, never letting go of her hand. She followed, an invasive chill seeping into every pore of her skin.

To her relief, the guest room appeared neat and clean, with fresh linens on the bed and a fireplace of its own. An antique mirrored dresser stood beside an equally old-fashioned four-poster bed. Gabriel's profile should have been clearly reflected to the left of her own, but she was puzzled to find his reflection blurry.

An effect of dust, or perhaps the silver had peeled away from the back, she decided. Yet her image, shimmering beside his, appeared clear and well defined.

Gabriel paid no attention to the mirror, or to her interest in it. He swept his open palm around in a half-circle. "Well, what do you think? It's been a while since anyone stayed over, and I'm not here all that often. I travel as much as possible, or take rooms at Purgatory or some comparable institution. Several of them are scattered around the world."

"And Caine?"

"Caine comes and goes. Sometimes years go by without any sign of him. Then, suddenly, he comes back to interfere in my life again."

"Why do you let him?"

"I told you. There's a bond between us. Nothing any human could comprehend."

She scoffed. "You make me sound like a different species."

"Deny it all you want. Tomorrow, when you spend the day here alone, you can think about what it all means."

"Alone? Where will you and Caine be?"

He smiled, but his jaw muscles stayed rigid. "Caine and I will be dead, of course—as we always are during the daylight hours. Now do you see the cause of my resentment? For almost two centuries, I haven't seen the sun, and if I survive for ten more centuries I won't see it again. He took that from me—simply so he could have a companion to ease his own loneliness."

"You must desire his company at some level—otherwise you wouldn't take him in."

"That's the blood bond. The sight of him infuriates me, but his absence drains me of the very will to survive. He's doomed me to an endless existence of misery. Still, I do appreciate one thing Caine did for me—finding you."

He slid his arms around her. His erection nudged her thighs. "We don't have a lot of time before the sun comes up. Still, we ought to finish what we started…and I would like to welcome you to my home properly."

He swept her up and settled her not onto the bed, as she'd expected, but up against the wall. Bracing her with one arm around her waist, Gabriel peeled off her tube-style dress and whisked away her panties in two swift, decisive motions. The garments pooled at her feet, leaving her only in her boots.

His own clothes followed hers to the floor within seconds—once again, his motions flowed too fast for her eyes to follow. She was exquisitely aware, however, of his right palm sliding up under her left thigh, raising it to the level of his hip. Melting into his caress, she hooked her knee around his waist and drew him into her heat.

Gabriel used his free hand to push her legs farther apart and then slipped it into the hot, wet channel between her thighs. Burrowing his first two fingers inside, he parted her wet folds and stroked her pulsating flesh until Lindsay thought she was about to turn inside out with need.

Moving deeper, his fingers found her throbbing center and slowly pulled back again to smear her free-flowing juices over her swollen outer lips. He kneaded her in a steady, rhythmic motion. Hot pleasure rolled through her in waves. Her thighs clasped and unclasped around his hand.

"Please, Gabriel…come inside me," she breathed. Crazy or not, she decided, his vampire game had drawn her all the way in. Whatever, whoever he was, she had never needed anything as much as she needed him to enter her. "I want you there."

His hand slid forward, the heel brushing her tender pearl. Her back arched, her pussy bucking toward him as if to take him in deeper.

Then, abruptly, his arm dropped to his side. The sudden loss of contact dragged a deep, shuddering gasp from her.

"Not yet," he growled. A moment later, something else rubbed her throbbing center—the tip of his cock, she realized with a shiver, which he was now guiding with that same lust-drenched hand. He wielded it like an artist's brush, dabbing and rubbing against her with just enough pressure to tease her into spasms.

Moments later, his erection slid inside her in a single, forceful thrust. His hips rocked upward with enough power to lift her completely off the floor. She moaned and wrapped both legs around his waist, forcing herself against him with every ounce of strength she could muster. The high heels of her boots scraped the backs of his thighs as she clung to his body like a wild creature clutching a storm-swept tree.

Desperately, his palms crept around to cup her buttocks. His long fingers pried her tender folds even farther apart, giving his cock full access to her depths. He plowed her, stretched her, pounded her burning flesh into jelly. When he couldn't force himself in another millimeter, he began a slow, agonizing withdrawal. Her breath escaped in a drawn-out moan that turned to a gasp of surprise as he pushed back inside with even greater vigor.

For the next few minutes, he gripped her butt and slid her up and down his length. Then she was coming, exploding, sparks of pleasure searing every inch of her. Her hair stood on end and her toes tingled inside her boots. She wasn't sure if she was screaming, squealing, or silent as the reality around her contracted into a single white-hot pinpoint of light.

Through it all, Gabriel's stamina never wavered, nor did he seem any closer to a climax of his own. If he did come, she remained too lost inside her own head to notice. All she knew was that eventually he retreated. One last flash of excitement flickered through her nervous system as he carried her over to the bed.

Gently, he unlaced her boots and flung them into the corner. Then he pulled back the covers, placed her inside, and settled himself on top of her.

"Those were a nice touch," he murmured, rubbing her legs. They still tingled in the aftermath of her Richter-scale orgasm. "Thank you."

"Gabriel...." she whispered, covering the round head of his cock with her palm. "You didn't come. Here...let me please you this time."

Without waiting for his response, she covered him with her hand, sliding up and down his length and circling his shaft with her tongue. His balls had already cooled and still felt firm to the touch. Lindsay cupped them in her fingers and rubbed them while he sighed in obvious enjoyment.

Just then the door flew open.

"I've started a fire. The house should be warm soon," Caine said casually, as if he'd intruded on nothing more intimate than a game of chess. "We don't have a lot of time, Gabriel." He ducked back out without waiting for a response.

Gabriel's mood changed. He disentangled himself from her and from the bedsheets and stood up, naked.

"You'll be alone until evening. We keep food in the pantry so our cleaning service won't get suspicious when they come in once a month, or on the off chance we have a human guest. Can you stoke the fire yourself?"

"Yes. At least, I'll do my best."

"Fair enough. We'll be back as soon as the sun sets."

"Where do you go?"

He smirked. "It wouldn't be wise of me to tell you. Caine and I are vulnerable during daylight hours."

"Do you think I would hurt you?"

"No, but I won't tempt you."

"How do you know I won't get in my car and drive away?" She wondered how much gas she had left. Where would she ever find a service station out here? How far could she get?

"You can if you wish. We'll see how well the blood-bond holds. Some humans can overcome it. Most can't."

"If you choose to stay, we'll talk in the evening." He paused in the middle of the room, reached down, and bobbled his cock in his hand. Lindsay gasped to find it already thick and hard again. "By the way, vampires don't come. Not in the way human guys do, anyway. I'm surprised you didn't figure that out by now."

He gathered up his clothes and walked out without putting them on. Exhausted, bewildered, but physically satisfied for the moment, Lindsay slept.

* * * *

When Lindsay awoke, daylight was streaming through the windows. Her overnight bag sat on the bureau next to her.

The prospect of spending another day alone didn't appeal to her, but at least she would have the run of the place for a few hours. Not knowing quite what to expect, she slid out of the comfortable guest bed and made her way down the uncarpeted hall.

Fortunately, Gabriel and Caine's vampire game didn't extend to turning their living space into a virtual tomb. She found a simple but functional bathroom with a huge tub and shower—both spotless, to her relief—and took a long, hot soak. Back in her room, she pulled on the jeans and sweatshirt again, grateful she'd had the presence of mind to bring them, and went off in search of nourishment.

On the first floor, a small kitchen opened into an even smaller pantry that stocked a few supplies. She made a pot of strong black tea and snacked on crackers smeared with peanut butter. Not much of a breakfast, but it would do.

Finally, refreshed and stoked with caffeine, Lindsay ventured outside to check on her car.

It sat in the same spot where Caine had parked, the keys still in the ignition and the doors unlocked. After sliding in, she sat in the driver's seat for a long time. Her GPS remained in its usual place clipped to the dashboard. When she tried to turn the unit on, it made a strange beeping sound and flickered off again. Either she was out of range or battery power. Inconvenient, but not insurmountable, assuming she had enough gas to get to any kind of a main road. Where exactly they were, of course, had yet to be determined.

Her hand crept toward the dashboard, but her fingertips stopped short of turning the key. A moment later, her wrist began to shake.

Was it academic curiosity that kept her from gunning the ignition? Or the feelings—akin to an addiction—she'd developed for them? Or the blood bond Caine had talked about?

Impossible, she reminded herself. She could leave any time she wanted to. Her subconscious was sending a message, all right, but it had nothing to do with vampires and brainwashing and things that went bump in the night. The fact remained that she had a lot of notes to commit to paper, and what better place to do it than in this quiet refuge, which contained no television or Internet to distract her?

Time to get started, before everything she'd so carefully memorized disappeared into her mental ether.

Back at the house, Lindsay began to explore, searching for the perfect room to immerse herself in work. Maybe she could also find out more about Caine and Gabriel in the process.

She entered every space she found—a long-unused dining room, an empty parlor, a spare bedroom filled with old furniture and trunks that contained nothing more controversial than old blankets and vintage clothing. All the hall closets stood empty, save for a few dusty overcoats and boots. Presumably Gabriel kept his own clothes in the master bedroom, which featured a locked wardrobe cabinet beside the king-sized, black-sheeted bed. She found nothing she could identify as belonging to Caine, either. Perhaps he stashed his personal possessions in whatever secret chamber he—or they—had retired to for the day.

At the end of the hall on the first floor, a locked metal door presumably led to an underground basement or storage area. Was this where they retreated to keep up their charade of avoiding sunlight? For their sake, she just hoped it wasn't infested with mold, rats, or other unpleasant features. The image made her shudder.

In a smaller room located just off the staircase, she found just the sort of workspace she'd dreamed of. Full bookcases lined three of the four walls, while the fourth consisted of a huge stone fireplace. Caine had kept his word—a steady blaze crackled in the grate, no doubt accounting for the house's more comfortable atmosphere this morning. An assortment of small logs lay to the right of the hearth. Lindsay cautiously fed one into the fire and stepped back to watch it flash and hiss as jagged tongues of flame consumed it.

The heat in the room grew thicker, wrapping her in a warm blanket of relaxed contentment. An old sofa in one corner yielded a few cushions that she artfully arranged in front of the fire, and the bookcases around her bulged with intellectual treats. She had all day—what was the rush in getting down to serious work?

She spent the next few hours reading old books, of which Gabriel owned an impressive number. Art history seemed a particular passion of his, and his collection featured several huge tomes with exquisite color plates depicting masterworks from the early 19th century. Most of the novels and volumes of poetry dated from the same era, including more than a few she suspected were rare collectibles. Many bore matching leather covers and bookplates featuring the name "Blackstone," suggesting that Gabriel had inherited them.

Conscious of their value, she handled the books gingerly before placing them back on the shelves. Though the arrangement seemed to follow no particular order, she was careful not to jumble them up. Still not ready to start her own work, she turned her attention to a closet set into one corner of the room. Unlike the others, this one remained unlocked, so full of odds and ends that the door wouldn't shut.

In the closet, she found stacks of paintings in antique frames, many of them featuring landscapes and still life. Though her experience in art was somewhat limited, she knew enough to recognize that these were not prints, but originals. The swipes of the artist's brush still showed in certain areas of the canvas, preserved in textured oils. Some featured the same name, "Blackstone." More relics of Gabriel's ancestors, she assumed, though she had only his word that he even owned the house. It might be a place the two men rented when they wanted to assume their vampire personas, or maybe it belonged to a friend, a relative, or someone else involved in the same lifestyle.

The largest painting leaned against the wall at the rear of the closet, its dust-smeared back to her. Since a virtual obstacle course of other odds and ends lay between her and it, she decided to forgo further exploration until later.

After tossing another log on the fire, she wandered back to the pantry and consumed her second ration of crackers and tea. If she stayed here, she would have to find a grocery store, though the prospect of a crash diet wasn't entirely unwelcome. No wonder Caine and Gabriel both looked so trim. Regular meals obviously weren't high on their priority list while they played their game. They were content to fast and sip from those ornate goblets in Purgatory.

As she munched, her thoughts returned to her research project. The details that had emerged about her target subculture both startled and intrigued her. When she'd put her initial plan together, she'd pegged the whole thing as an elaborate sexual fetish, not unlike the underground bondage clubs or swingers' societies some of her psychologist colleagues had written about. Now she realized there were dimensions she hadn't considered.

A trip back to the guest room yielded her notebook and a pen. On a whim, she grabbed the bedspread, too, and carried everything downstairs. Soon she was stretched out in front of the fire, lying on her stomach with the open notebook on the floor.

Once again, the words wouldn't flow, so she contented herself with drawing a few doodles, which became steadily more ornate until she began to write in earnest. She jotted down her impressions of Purgatory, the scenes of debauchery she'd witnessed, the absolute conviction of the participants that they were in fact vampires. They wore costumes connecting them to their favorite historical eras and feasted on an unknown substance that symbolized human blood. Aiding them in their play-acting were people who preferred the role of victim, or "donor," as Caine and Gabriel referred to them. The tasting of blood regularly enhanced sex acts between the participants.

While she scribbled on, her mind chasing words that remained maddeningly elusive, the heat from the fire grew more intense. Soon she closed her eyes and drifted into a pleasant fantasy of Caine and Gabriel running their hands over her back and shoulders. Before long, their touch became intimate, sliding under her clothes, teasing her nipples and the moistening thatch between her legs. While one hand pinched and tugged, the other began a slow incursion between her puffy labial folds, gliding along on her own natural lubricant.

Short bursts of delight pulsed through her with every stroke of their fingers. Stretching her limbs, she relaxed into a seductive dream of pleasure.

She wasn't sure how much time passed before she awoke, disoriented. She looked out the window. Gray storm clouds had moved from the sea and clustered over the house. The sun was nowhere to be seen. The air felt colder now, though her skin felt flushed and damp. The muscles between her legs throbbed as if she'd just enjoyed a wonderful orgasm...but couldn't remember any of it.

Her notebook had fallen from her hands and the pen had rolled across the hearth to lie balanced between two bricks. When she reached over to pick it up, her gaze fell on what she had written earlier—what should have been the outline for the opening chapter of her study.

She couldn't make out a single legible word. Bizarre, looping squiggles filled the entire lined page. To her astonishment, she realized she'd dreamed all the writing she'd done.

Heaving herself to her feet, she grabbed a few more logs from the hearth and tossed them into the fire. They didn't catch as easily this time. The flame flickered and sputtered before leveling out to a slow burn. Why did she have so much trouble focusing lately?

Lindsay looked around the room at the shelves of old books and the paintings she'd rescued from the closet. Something nagged at the back of her mind—something she'd intended to do before she'd drifted off.

The closet. Yes. She'd been planning to get the largest of the paintings out of the closet. Until she accomplished that task, she decided, she couldn't hope to get any real work done. Her curiosity about what lay on the opposite side of that canvas affected her ability to concentrate. That explained the mess in the notebook.

Systematically, she made her way through the jumble of boxes, crates, and old furniture. The canvas was so big she had to slide the frame all the way out of the closet before she could turn it over to view it.

She drew in a breath. This was no landscape or artistically arranged jumble of pottery. Instead, she found herself looking at a lushly detailed portrait of three figures. Even in their posed state, stiff in the formal dress of a bygone era, the woman and two men in the painting seemed intimately bonded to one another. The woman's hand rested on the shoulder of the man to her right, while her eyes turned to the companion on her left. The artist had perfectly captured the emotional tension that crackled between the three of them.

The date in the corner of the canvas read "1880," and beside it curled the same signature as before—"Blackstone." Lindsay had no idea who the woman might have been, but she had no doubt about the men's identities. A hundred and thirty years had passed, but Caine and Gabriel hadn't changed at all.

Chapter 7

At the sound of someone entering the room, Lindsay let the painting drop against the wall.

Caine stood in a black silk dressing gown. She doubted he wore anything underneath. A triangle of pale, waxy skin showed above the open v-shape at his chest. His damp hair smelled fresh from a shower.

His eyes darkened when his gaze slanted toward the painting.

"Foolish woman. That was one door better left closed, literally."

"I only wanted to—"

He took her face in both hands and tilted it to his. "Never mind. I must feed now."

His thumbs stroked the underside of her chin, melting her anxiety. Was he hypnotizing her?

"Yes," she repeated, her thoughts beginning to drift. She absorbed his hunger. It felt like a rodent gnawing her stomach while a velvet glove caressed the same spot. In her case, it wasn't blood she craved. "Time to feed."

"I haven't hurt you yet," he purred. His index finger glided to her lips and stroked them softly apart. She curled her tongue around his fingertip and suckled. "Why would I do so now?"

"You won't," she whispered when he drew his hand away and unlashed his robe. It fell open to free his straining erection.

Placing both hands on his chest, Lindsay leaned in and began to kiss her way down the front of his body. While she sank, he lifted her sweatshirt over her head, allowing her bare breasts to slide along his taut abdomen and groin. His muscles trembled in anticipation.

She ended up on her knees in front of him, her full lips sheathing the cool pillar between his thighs. Caine growled in pleasure, threading his fingers through her hair. His hands guided her head as she bobbed up and down the length of his stalk, starting with slow, drawn-out movements and then moving faster. Finally, he pushed her all the way onto his thick cock, filling her throat. Her face nestled against his shower-dampened pubes as she curled her tongue around his shaft, enticing warmth and life through the barely pulsing veins.

Soon the muscles clenched beneath his frosty skin. Caine's torso went rigid and his fingers ground her scalp with unexpected force. A burst of heat seemed to suffuse his body—or at least that portion of it still jammed into her mouth. A deep, low gurgle issued from his chest.

When he tugged free of her, she looked up at a very different kind of man than the one who'd loomed up behind her only minutes before. This one had a healthy, living glow in his eyes and on his cheeks. His hands, too, relaxed in her hair and dropped to her shoulders. He balanced himself against her as he sank to the floor beside her.

One part of him didn't soften. Still as rigid and hard as a column of stone, his cock seemed larger than ever as it curved out from his hips. The plump head nudged her left breast and bumped her side as he crouched down.

The quilt she'd spread out earlier invited them to stretch out on top. Caine shed his robe, slid her jeans over her hips, and tossed them aside. He rolled her onto her back and positioned himself on top of her without a single word or even an unspoken signal. They moved together by instinct, sharing one body and one train of thought. He hadn't embellished the truth when he had spoken of the connection between them. A blood-bond, he'd called it, but she suspected it reached far deeper. At some primal level, they were made for one another.

He entered her in a single, perfectly centered thrust. A jolt of heat now spread through her, just as it had for him moments earlier. Her willing muscles caught him, squeezed him, and held him in place. When he rocked his pelvis upward, he lifted her off the floor with him. Lindsay wanted to stay that way indefinitely, with Caine's rhythmic thrusts edging her closer and closer to the very edge of ecstasy, but never quite toppling her over.

Just then her self-control imploded in a burst of total, mind-obliterating joy. A searing flame rushed from the center of her body all the way to the roots of her hair and the ends of her toes. The room tilted and blurred, and her flesh turned to liquid fire.

Caine's teeth entered the side of her throat, reopening the exact same punctures he had made before. The sensation spurred her to a higher level of bliss.

He took only as much blood as he needed. When he pulled his mouth away and slid his cock from her body, she sensed pure contentment in his thoughts.

Equally sated, the two of them slumped onto the quilt. Caine remained on top of her, using his weight as a makeshift blanket. Lindsay wrapped her arms around him, pulling him close. The warmth she'd given him flowed back into her through his touch.

Though her vision was still hazy, she became aware of another figure entering the room and moving to stand beside their huddled forms. When her eyes focused, they registered Gabriel's booted feet against the wooden floor. She shifted to look up at him. Unlike Caine, he'd started to get dressed, though his blue jeans remained enticingly unzipped, and his white shirt hung unbuttoned. She was less gratified when his hands curled into fists at his sides.

He wasn't staring at the two of them, however. His attention was directed at the portrait that still leaned against the wall.

"Why did you show her my painting?" he demanded of Caine, who reluctantly disentangled himself from her limbs and sat up on the blanket.

"Why shouldn't she see it? It's part of who we are."

"Yes, it certainly is." Gabriel's mouth twisted in barely contained rage. "Did you tell her the full story, Caine?"

"He didn't tell me anything," Lindsay volunteered. As curious as his outburst made her, she didn't want to touch off an argument. "I didn't ask him. I took the painting out of the closet."

"And I will put it back," Caine said, rising. He pulled on his dressing gown, picked up the unwieldy frame in one hand, and returned it to its hiding place. He shut the closet door for good measure. "Happy now?"

Gabriel responded with a grunt.

"You need to feed." Caine slid his hands into the pockets of his robe and leaned against the wall. "You'll feel much better when you do."

"Not yet. I'm not in the mood."

"All right, then. I'll let you think of some other way to entertain our guest. I would say I've already done my part this evening."

Lindsay shifted uncomfortably under the quilt. Gabriel retrieved her discarded clothes and tossed them to her. She pulled them on, aware of their hawk-like gazes following her every move.

"Well?" Gabriel asked when she stood, dressed again. "I'm sure I won't be able to live up to Caine's example, but what would you consider an adequate way to pass the evening?"

"I don't know," she admitted. Discussing their plans like a trio of college students heading off-campus on a Friday night struck her as odd. "How do you usually amuse yourselves without Internet or TV?"

"The same way people did for thousands of years before those things were invented," Caine said. "We might spend a few hours with a good book, or engaged in conversation—not to mention the more basic activities that have sustained humanity through the centuries."

"I hope you're not one of those modern types who panics if the electricity goes out for a few hours," Gabriel ventured. "Because sometimes that happens."

"Of course not. I mean, I wouldn't enjoy sitting in the dark, but I'm not addicted to video games or anything. In fact, when I was in college, a friend took me to a meeting of the Medieval Society. One weekend a month, they devoted themselves to recreating life in the Middle Ages, complete with homemade suits of armor and tankards of ale around a bonfire."

"Sounds like a perfect cover for vampires." Caine laughed. "The rest of those poseurs would have lasted about an hour in the real past."

"As far as I know, there weren't any vampires." On reflection, the students weren't so different from the clientele at Purgatory. Both Caine and the woman with the colorful drinks referred to the foul man who attacked her as a relic from the thirteenth century. Their fantasies differed in degree, rather than in kind, from the nerdy young men who jousted with cardboard lances behind the football stadium.

"Or at least they didn't reveal themselves to you."

"Perhaps you're right," she conceded and let the matter drop. Privately, she filed the comparison away as a possible avenue for further study. Judging by the lengths someone had gone to in making the painting look antique, nostalgia was an integral part of the scene. Perhaps they imagined life as more exciting or fulfilling in earlier centuries. Or perhaps claiming to be hundreds of years old was an attempt to impress others.

"You know what the main difference is between the way things were then and the way they are now?" Gabriel mused. "The silence. Today, you can't go anywhere without hearing music blaring or cell phones going off. Modern people don't even think about the noise cars and planes make. Those things have always been part of your world, just like hoofbeats were for me and Caine."

Caine nodded. "It's all a matter of what you're trained to filter out."

"I suppose that's true." The house did seem abnormally still. Except for their voices, the old-fashioned clock on the mantel provided the only sound. No wonder she'd felt so lazy and out of sorts all afternoon. Background noise could make things seem normal, uncomfortable, or even threatening, all via the subconscious.

"I used to look for ways to fill that silence," Gabriel continued, his voice taking on an edge. "In the old days, gypsies used to camp in the woods. I started by inviting groups of them in to help me pass the endless nights. Eventually, I discovered others like me. I threw parties here that made the back rooms at Purgatory look like meetings of the Royal Philosophical Society."

"Gypsies?" Lindsay doubted that. Still, Joel had told her about communities of drug addicts and social misfits camping out in rustic spots where civilization and the law wouldn't disturb them. Perhaps they, too, had become part of Gabriel's fantasy life.

"Of course." Caine grinned at the memory. "Not the most intellectual companions, but we had to have someone to…ah…feast with. And the music was lively. They fled as soon as the snow melted."

"That was a long time ago, though," Gabriel said. "Now I prefer the quiet. You're the first guest we've had in years, Lindsay. But I'm glad you're here."

"I am, too." Lindsay met his eyes and smiled.

"Why don't we indulge in another antiquated pastime?" Caine suggested. "And before anyone accuses me of ungentlemanly conduct, I am referring to an evening walk around the grounds."

"In the dark?" Lindsay asked.

"Of course. Gabriel and I could join you at no other time. You might be surprised how much you miss by limiting yourself to sunlit excursions. Wait one moment, and I'll be delighted to show you."

He left her alone with Gabriel, who grunted and tucked in his shirt. Lindsay, meanwhile, began to look around for her shoes. She found them at opposite ends of the room, tossed aside while she and Caine were flailing about. She hid her blush as she sat on the floor and tugged them on.

"The isolation here doesn't bother you?" she asked him. "It must get pretty desolate in the winter."

"I actually prefer solitude. True, feeding is more difficult, but I've learned to plan ahead. Caine hates the bottled stuff, but he makes do while he's around. The main thing is safety. When the house is buried under six feet of snow, no one can disturb us. And, in turn, the humans are safe from us."

Lindsay busied herself with her shoelaces. Their masks never slipped, not even for a second. "I see."

"You might have gotten the wrong idea before." Gabriel paced the room, buttoning his shirt cuffs. "You need to know that I've never killed anyone, Lindsay. Not when I was human, not since I became what I am now. I've taken blood from plenty of people, and, I admit, not all of them were willing. But I never harmed a single soul, I swear."

"I...I guess I'm glad to hear that."

"Caine, on the other hand—"

He stopped abruptly as the man himself re-entered the room. His silk, dove-gray shirt, creased dark slacks, and pointed dress shoes seemed more suited to a nightclub than a tramp through the woods, but she considered that a good sign. Caine's idea of a walk, even at night, apparently revolved around decorum rather than adventure. He wouldn't expect her to climb rocks or navigate brambles.

Caine offered a gentlemanly arm at the front door. She accepted, mostly from a desire to avoid stumbling down the steps in the dark. Behind them, she heard Gabriel's grumble of disapproval.

They crossed the driveway and headed into a shadowy thicket of trees. Caine strolled along the threadlike path confidently, as if it were broad daylight. Gabriel trailed a few paces behind them, saying nothing.

"I can hear the ocean, but I can't see it," Lindsay observed, tilting her head in the direction of the distant but familiar whisper of the waves.

"Just over that ridge." Caine pointed to something she couldn't make out and pulled her along with him. Moments later, they had threaded their way past the tree line and stood atop a jagged cliff. Thirty feet below, the icy sea raged, its frothy peaks illuminated by an amber half-moon. Ahead of them, a weather-beaten gazebo perched on the tallest of the rocks.

Despite her misgivings, Lindsay had to admit that she found the sheer, raw beauty of the spot awe-inspiring. The hum of nocturnal creatures, the complex web of shadows, and the fresh scent of the ocean had a vaguely intoxicating effect on her.

Gabriel climbed into the gazebo and leaned on the rail. "Come inside," he called, holding out a hand to her. She glanced at Caine, who nodded and dropped her arm.

Cold wind and a faint salt spray stroked her face. She clasped the gazebo railing gingerly, afraid the thin planks might fracture under the pressure.

"Don't worry," Gabriel said. He slid his arms around her from behind, locking them under her breasts and resting his chin on her shoulder. "It's anchored down securely, and the wood's sturdy enough. We won't fly off into the surf."

She forced herself to relax into his embrace, though she knew Caine was watching them from his spot on the ground.

"Tell me...what do you do in the real world?" Gabriel asked. "I assume, like most modern women, you have a career of some kind."

"I...I work in a library," she said. It wasn't exactly a lie. The long hours she put in at the campus, shuffling through research materials, surely counted as a vocational pursuit.

"Hence your interest in vampires? You came across the old legends in books, perhaps?"

"Well...yes. I have done a lot of reading on the subject."

Gabriel nodded. "Makes sense. Many people come to know vampires through the printed word. They find out soon enough that most written accounts are exaggerated, or distorted almost beyond recognition."

"I'm sure."

"We could set the record straight if we chose, but as you know, the community prefers secrecy." His hands moved along the front of her body, languidly bringing her simmering heat to the surface. "Tell me...do you have a lover? In the human world, I mean."

"No." A warm sweat broke out on her forehead. "I mean, there was a man once...in college. Our relationship didn't work out. He left me."

"That hurt you."

"Yes. Very much." Lindsay found herself startled by her own honesty, considering how much else she'd learned to fib about. Somehow, Gabriel had touched a particularly sensitive spot in her psyche.

"He was a fool, then. I'm glad."

Gabriel bent lower, running his lips down the curve of her neck. The flat of his tongue stroked the same path, darting in rhythm with her quickening pulse. The slight graze of his teeth stirred the usual rush of physical desire. Lindsay readied herself for a more intimate connection.

His hardness swelled against the back of her thigh, prompting her to grope for his zipper. She found his thick, denim-covered mound and began to knead. Gabriel moaned, pressing his mouth deeper into the hollow between her throat and shoulder.

Then, with the speed and fluidity of a sea wind changing course, he stepped back and away from her.

"No. I don't want to feed on you. I can't."

"Why not?" Before her lips had finished moving, Gabriel had gone. She caught a glimpse of his silhouetted form, stalking off through the trees and then disappearing from sight.

How had he moved so quickly? The powerful mixture of night air and hormones must be toying with her senses. Caine hadn't been joking about the darkness bringing on new experiences.

"His petulance is becoming tiresome," Caine said, offering his hand and helping her down the gazebo steps. "He'll be better once he feeds."

"It's all right. I'm a little overwhelmed myself."

Caine turned her hand upward and placed something small and delicate in the center of her palm. Lindsay looked down to find a paper-thin white flower, its milky petals spread like the powdery wings of some exotic moth. The breeze made it seem to pulse in her hand.

"In case you desired further confirmation that beautiful things do bloom at night," he said, cradling her fingers in his.

"I never doubted it. This is lovely. The flower and the walk. I understand now why you don't get bored."

"Dangers lurk, too. Never forget." He dropped her hand. "You said you wanted to learn about us, and you've been an enthusiastic pupil thus far. Gabriel and I have plenty more to teach you. But first, I must ask you a question. Could you love him?"

She blinked. "You mean Gabriel?"

"Yes, of course. Who else?"

"I expected you to ask if I could love you."

"Immaterial at the moment. If you can, well and good. Gabriel is my first concern. You see how he is. I can survive without the softer emotions intruding on my life. He cannot."

"Does that mean you would reject love?"

His jaw stiffened. "We are not speaking of me, but of Gabriel. Have you an answer?"

Lindsay frowned. Certainly she found Gabriel physically appealing, not to mention sexually exciting. Caine was both of those things, too. How could she ever consider forming deeper emotions with a man—or even two men—whose entire identity was based on at best, a fantasy, and at worst, a deliberate lie?

"I'd...have to say it's a bit too soon to decide," she compromised. "I don't know enough about him...about either of you."

"Time will remedy that." He motioned for her to accompany him. "I want you to go to him now. He needs to feed. The painting represents many things that disturb him."

"I'm sorry," Lindsay said as they started back toward the house, Caine walking just behind her. "I didn't realize my pulling it out would cause such a ruckus."

"Never mind. He needs to face his emotions where that subject is concerned. A single century of brooding is more than enough, in my opinion."

His take on psychoanalysis amused her. Yet Caine had a point. Whatever had happened between Gabriel and the woman in the painting had damaged him emotionally, perhaps shaking his commitment to his vampiric delusions. Lindsay felt certain she could help him work through his misgivings, or at least begin the process. Not only would a successful outcome provide the perfect final chapter for her dissertation, it would be a good way to get her feet wet—putting aside all other body parts for the moment—as a psychologist.

Chapter 8

"I know the painting upsets him, which is why I stashed it in the closet in the first place," Caine said as they walked back to the house. "It reminds him not only of what he lost, but what he once was."

"Do you mean…human?"

"No. He was already a vampire when he painted that." Noting her surprise, he nodded. "It's true. He was once a most promising artist with an eternity to perfect his talent, but he gave up. Pity. I bear some responsibility for his choice."

"I understand you bear responsibility for a lot of things."

"No doubt Gabriel has told you plenty of tales about me. Don't you think my perspective might be different?"

"I'm sure it is." She shivered as his overly bright eyes raked her face. "The woman in the painting—tell me about her."

"Her name was Piletta. She was well-known in high society for her quick tongue and decisive manner, rare qualities in women of her era. Gabriel and I were frequent visitors to a particular salon where she often held sway. Such places might be considered precursors to venues like Purgatory."

"Places for vampires, you mean." Lindsay marveled at the smooth manner in which he rattled off the story. The painting had to be a fake, but they had certainly gone to a lot of trouble to create a plausible history for it and the people it depicted. "You went looking for victims?"

"An unfortunate term, not to mention inaccurate. Then, as now, we preferred to call them 'donors.' Piletta wasn't our victim."

Lindsay was inclined to believe him. The woman in the painting was clearly no shrinking violet. The tilt of her head and the overtly seductive flame in her gaze suggested someone who would go with the two men willingly, just as Lindsay herself had.

"So what happened?"

"I got rid of her. I had good reason. She was trying to destroy Gabriel. And I don't mean trying to manipulate his emotions, or erode his self-esteem, or any such modern psychobabble. I mean attempting to drive a stake through his heart and set him on fire while he was lying in bed. If I hadn't intervened…."

Lindsay shuddered. No wonder Gabriel was having second thoughts about these vampire games. They could easily get out of hand when the participants became too enmeshed in the more lurid trappings.

"Piletta's loss affected us both very deeply for a very long time, and still does," Caine went on. "However much Gabriel wants to blame me, or hate me for what I did, the bottom line is that he owes his continued existence to me."

"What did Gabriel say when you told him what happened? Wouldn't he feel at least some gratitude toward you for…ah…saving him?"

"Gabriel has never been one to feel gratitude of any sort, much less express any. If anything, he believes I need to earn his forgiveness. After a hundred and twenty-five years, I have not."

"You mean he doesn't know the whole story behind what happened? Your actions were meant to save him. It sounds to me like you need to talk about it…to explain the situation."

Lindsay cringed inwardly at how impossibly lame she sounded. Still, how else could she respond? Psychoanalytic literature stressed that arguing with the deluded was a waste of time, and therapy for self-proclaimed vampires probably followed the same pattern it did for mortals.

"Frankly, I don't mind letting him believe I was at fault. His life was already hard enough, thanks to me. He didn't need to be disillusioned yet again. You see, Gabriel may have loved Piletta. But she loved me. Her plan was to dispose of Gabriel so she and I could be together. I wasn't prepared to make such a choice. How could I tell him, though? If he hated me before..."

They reached the house. Caine held the front door open while she slipped inside. "I told him as much as I could bear to," he went on. "The rest will have to remain locked inside me. You may find that hard to understand, but I don't care what you think of me. I simply want Gabriel to be happy." His eyes held genuine pain.

"Is that supposed to be my role in this? You think I can give him peace?"

"Yes. From the time I first saw you, I sensed you had the ability to reach him. Empathy is something few humans and even fewer vampires possess. You sensed it, too, the moment you met him, didn't you?"

"Yes," she admitted. "The connection existed before he said a word to me."

"Perhaps that is what mortals mean when they talk about finding their soul mates. By definition, a vampire can experience no such thing. However, Gabriel's response to you was more than I dared hope for." Caine thrust his hands into his pockets. "Everything to this point may be considered amusement, a way for Gabriel and me to pass a few sweet days as we travel toward eternity. What comes next must be far more meaningful. Go to him. Ease his pain. His existence—and quite possibly yours— depends on your success."

He made no attempt to follow as she made her way upstairs in search of Gabriel.

She'd guessed correctly—Gabriel lay in the huge bed that dominated the master bedroom. His face was glum, his denim-clad knees drawn against his chest. He looked up when she lingered in the open doorway.

"Caine forced you into coming up here, didn't he?"

"He didn't," Lindsay assured him. "I'm here, in this room, because I want to be."

"Hmm." Gabriel settled his shoulders back against the headboard and raked a hand through his tousled gold hair. "You know I need to feed soon. You're not afraid to be alone with me?"

She was about to deny it, but decided to be honest. "Of course, a little. But neither of you has hurt me yet. Why would you start now?"

Moving so quickly that his limbs became a blur, Gabriel reached up and pulled her to him. He cocooned her with his legs and slid his arms under hers, peeling her sweatshirt off in a single, brisk motion. She trailed her hands along his chest, pushing back the loose flaps of his shirt. She saw his pupils flare as his gaze settled on the curve of her exposed throat.

"So soft and white," he whispered. His voice sounded vague, almost mesmerized by the sight. He leaned over as if to kiss her, but stopped and drew back.

"No," he said, shaking his head with determination. "I can fight the urge for now. The situation won't get desperate for a few more days." He tilted his head and brushed his fingers over her drying puncture wounds. "You sound as though you want me to do this. Have you started to enjoy it?"

"I... don't know how to answer. I suppose the bite itself scares me a little. But the connection that goes with it...when we come together...it's like nothing I've ever experienced."

"Yes. I remember what it was like. Funny—when I was alive, back when such things weren't talked about and young people were kept ignorant until marriage—human orgasm seemed the most miraculous thing I had ever discovered. As you now know, though, it's nothing at all compared to what happens when your blood flows into me. In that moment, for as long as it lasts, I'm fully, wonderfully alive again. I might resent Caine for a lot of things, but I can't fault him for teaching me how to combine sex and feeding."

"Is that why you and Caine still…you know…team up?" Strange. She'd given both men free use of her body, access to her mind and maybe even her soul, but she still hesitated to refer to their three-way physical relationship out loud.

"Biting is easier when the person is coming. The flesh is softer, the blood sweeter. Since it's difficult to manage both at the same time, we learned how to switch off."

"I see." She fought back a blush, but knew the heat was spreading down her whole body. Gabriel's eyes traveled between her breasts, following the rosy tide with obvious appreciation.

"You'll notice some real changes soon," he continued. "Your strength will increase. Your hearing and sight will sharpen. Any wounds you sustain will heal faster. Best of all, you'll live longer and age slowly. The longer you keep feeding me, the more benefits you'll reap. That's why so many humans long to become our donors, and why most of us don't accept just anyone. She has to be special."

The obvious question rose to her lips before she could suppress it.

"Like the woman in the painting? Was she special in the same way I am? And was she the one who showed you how to…ah…work together?"

"Piletta was unique for a woman of her time. She had no problem recognizing and taking what she wanted, including men. But in the way you mean, no. She was nothing like you."

His obvious pain, kept in check by a veneer of barely suppressed rage, told her not to press the issue further.

"Would you like me to please you?" she asked instead.

"Is that what you want?" His tone had grown flat, almost indifferent.

"Yes," she said, flattening her palms on his chest. "It is."

He arched his back toward her, pushing himself against her hands, squeezing her between his strong thighs. His hard muscles tensed under his ashen flesh.

Her fingers swept the tails of his shirt behind his hips and moved on to the band of his jeans. She worked the button and zipper open, exposing a soft cloud of champagne-colored hair. A slight tug freed his erection, which curved up against her hand to nuzzle her like a curious animal. She coaxed it to its full, hard length with firm strokes while Gabriel watched her with a detached expression.

Nestling herself between his legs, Lindsay rested her face against his thigh and molded her lips to the sleek curve of his cool sac. Her tongue teased his fuzz-tufted base and slithered upward to encircle his crown. He moaned when she lapped him gently, using her lower lip to massage the underside of his shaft.

After a few moments, she settled her knees around his hips. Grasping his shoulders for balance, she raised herself enough to catch his cockhead in the crevice between her thighs. Her folds were still tender from Caine's vigorous invasion, yet already moist and eager to be breached again. When Gabriel's cock tip pushed against her clitoris and started to burrow inside, Lindsay shuddered as if he'd suddenly penetrated all the way to her core.

Murmuring with enjoyment, she pressed forward again, her needy center trapping and then swallowing his cock. Rigid yet cool, it probed inside her like a length of steel thrust into a furnace. Instantly, her heat began to thaw him. The thunderous clash of fire and ice sent bolts of excitement winging through her.

His body felt warmer and more supple now. He sank inside her even more deeply than before. Her inner muscles clenched, captured, and massaged him. Their consummation was so complete that for a few intoxicating moments she forgot about everything outside Gabriel's room, his bed, his firm cock filling her to bursting.

She hovered for what seemed like eternity, deliciously close to the sweet implosion she remembered and craved so completely. She knew perfectly well what final spark was needed to ignite both of them.

Gabriel knew, too. His fingers dug into her upper arms and hauled her to him in a single, desperate motion. Lindsay felt his teeth scrape along her left shoulder, his tongue rasping over the half-healed lesions on her throat. A simple twist of his head and the tightening of his jaw would be enough to join them in ecstasy.

Then, in as little time as it would have taken him to break her skin with his fangs, he pushed her away and rolled to his feet.

"No. I won't, I can't. Not when the temptation is this strong. The way I am now…I know I'd hurt you."

He crossed the room in three long strides, fastening his jeans as he went. After opening the door of his wardrobe, he extracted a dressing gown similar to the one Caine wore and tossed it onto the bed next to her. "Perhaps later…when I've regained control of my emotions."

"Gabriel—wait!" Her skin burned with humiliation and her pulse raced with unsatisfied desire. Without a backward glance at her, Gabriel stormed from the room and slammed the door behind him.

After he'd gone, Lindsay remained motionless on the bed in an awkward heap, like a swimmer who had been caught in a sudden maelstrom at sea and violently deposited on a rocky shoal. Her vision blurred, her head buzzed, and every muscle in her legs and torso ached. Still, she forced herself to turn onto her side and pushed her arms into the sleeves of the dressing gown. It took more time before she could comfortably stand, and making her way down the stairs proved an exercise in physical discomfort. Yet staying in his large, cold room alone seemed an even less appealing prospect.

"Gabriel?" she called softly.

She spotted him in the small sitting room. He had pulled the painting out again and propped it against the side of the sofa. He stood in front of it, legs apart and arms folded, scrutinizing it like a critic in a museum.

"Come and sit with me," he said, never diverting his gaze from the canvas.

"The fire's low," she said, moving toward the hearth and stretching her hands out in front of it. "I wasn't sure how much wood to add this afternoon. I didn't want to cause a fire or anything."

He swung around, his arms dropping to his sides. He studied the wilting flame as though he were noticing it for the first time. "I know a way to make it roar again. I could burn my painting. The oils would melt almost at once, and the canvas would follow. The frame might last an hour or two. What do you think?"

"I don't know," she said, taken aback by the intensity of his voice and the determined glow in his eyes. "It seems sort of a waste."

"I suppose that might be a consideration." Gabriel stroked the stubble on his chin in thought. "After all, there will never be another Blackstone painting."

"I know. Caine says you don't paint anymore."

"He's right." His eyes hardened and slid away from hers. "The man who created that portrait no longer exists."

"But the detail in your painting—it goes beyond skill. The woman—it's almost as though she's standing in this room with us. You brought her to life."

"Rather ironic, considering I was responsible for her death, too."

"She's dead? I'm sorry—I hadn't realized that. Caine simply told me she was gone."

"She's gone, all right." He laughed bitterly. "What did you think he meant?"

"Is that why you gave up your art? Because you lost her?"

"She wasn't the only reason." Stepping forward, he picked up a brass poker and slowly stirred the ash. A few dull sparks leapt and then faded under his prodding. "I don't want to get into the details right now. Let's just say too much has happened. Too much has changed."

"Are you sure? I mean…you have such talent, Gabriel. Why let it go to waste?"

"Because I'm not an artist. I'm a fraud." He flung the poker back against the stones. "An artist needs a soul, and I'm pretty sure I don't have one. You know that."

"I'm not in a position to judge the state of anyone's soul. How can you?"

"Because I can feel the hole in my chest where it's supposed to be. Maybe it's like when people lose a limb—they say they can still sense its presence. But when they try to use it, the lack becomes all the more apparent. That's what it's like for me, all the time. You can't even imagine the kind of torture I go through on a daily basis."

Lindsay started to reach for him, but the raw agony in his expression stopped her. Touching him now, she suspected, might unleash a reaction she wasn't prepared to deal with just yet.

"But if you had no soul, how could you know pain? You'd be a shell, a collection of moving body parts, and nothing more. I see so much more when I look at you. And I sense a lot more when we're together. You say you can't produce art any longer, but can't you still recognize beauty? Isn't that a place to start?"

"Yes." His voice sank to a husky growl. She thought she saw the flicker of moisture in the corners of his eyes. "I see beauty when I look at you. That's partly why I don't want to feed on you any more. You are not simply a means to an end for me. I want us to know one another—really know one another."

"I want the same thing." She paused. "You know, Gabriel, this house could be beautiful, too, if only you cared about it enough."

"Well, I don't."

"Why not?"

"It's a place to stay. To exist. Not to live."

"Caine doesn't feel that way."

"Caine likes being the way he is. He brought me into this with him."

"How did you meet?"

Gabriel shrugged. "He had an interesting face. I wanted to paint him. He agreed. When the painting was done, we became friends. We shared women even then. He took me to a brothel in Boston." He laughed bitterly. "I didn't understand my role in it until the first time I saw him feed." His face tightened. "How does it make you feel—serving both of us like that?"

"When I came to Purgatory, I was searching for something. You and Caine have given it to me. We really are bonded. If my blood can give you peace…if it's a gift I can give you, then I'm happy to."

He didn't answer.

"Would it matter if I told you that Caine had a reason to come between you and Piletta?"

"Of course he did. That's simple enough. He wanted her gone. He wanted power over me. It's been the same story with him for a hundred and fifty years."

Lindsay took a deep breath. This time, she did take a step closer to him. "That isn't what he told me."

"You and he discussed what happened?" Gabriel's pupils flared, then narrowed. She saw his shoulders tense and his hands draw in to his sides.

"Yes, we did. Why does that seem strange to you?"

He gaped at her, his outrage fading into bewilderment. "Because in all these years…he never has."

"We all have secrets, Gabriel. As irrational as our behavior seems, we keep our biggest ones from the people we care most about."

A sudden chill passed through the room, prickling the skin on her arms. A moment later, she realized the cause.

Caine had reappeared.

"How true that we all have secrets. And how thoughtful of you to betray mine when I am not present. Before you unburden yourself on my behalf, though, perhaps you would care to share some of your own."

Chapter 9

"What makes you think I have secrets?" Lindsay struggled to keep her voice level.

Caine leaned against the door jamb, scowling. "Everyone has secrets. Besides, I've tasted your blood several times now. I've learned to recognize the bitterness of deception."

The faint choking sensation in the back of her throat intensified. She started to protest, but to her surprise, Caine let the matter drop.

"Never mind. I'm tired of all these emotional gymnastics. Whatever you have hidden from us will come out eventually. We can deal with the consequences then." He flashed Gabriel a look of disdain. "And to think I fed lightly just so you could indulge. That should be the last time I do you such a favor, though I doubt it shall be."

"Please yourself," Gabriel shot back.

Caine stepped closer to Lindsay, resting one hand on her shoulder and the other under her chin. He tipped her head up, gazing into her eyes with such intensity that she suddenly grew faint.

"You look tired, Lindsay. It's late by daywalker standards, and I did take some of your blood. You should rest now. Gabriel and I will find other ways to amuse ourselves until dawn."

"Tired...yes." Though she struggled to keep them open, her eyelids began to droop, as if someone had taped tiny weights to them. Her limbs became thick and almost too heavy to move. Even her pulse slowed to a sluggish thrum in her veins.

She was conscious of Caine's hand leaving her face, while the other slipped lower around her shoulders. Her feet left the floor as he caught her under the knees and hoisted her into his arms. Though her vision was blurry and her mind was wandering, she had the impression of floating upstairs.

"Sleep now," Caine said when he lowered her again.

"Sleep…yes," she murmured as a comforting softness and warmth closed in around her. The guest bed swallowed her up.

* * * *

In the morning, Lindsay awoke determined to spend the coming hours more productively than she had the day before. First and foremost, she decided to get something substantial to eat. Another day munching on crackers and sipping tea was out of the question. A couple of new t-shirts and a new pair of jeans wouldn't hurt, either, though she doubted she'd find a mall among the evergreens.

Both guys had disappeared again, which gave her enough time and freedom to carry out her plan. After stuffing her dirty laundry in her overnight bag, she walked out to the driveway and settled into the driver's seat. Her keys were still in the ignition, and she had enough gas in her car to tool around until she found a place to top off the tank.

An odd, sinking sensation gripped her stomach as she pulled down the driveway and out onto the gravel road. The urge to turn around and re-enter the house became so strong that her foot strayed toward the brake in anticipation of hooking a sudden U-turn. Her gnawing hunger and need for coffee, though, won out.

If she hadn't known better, she would have thought the house—or the men hiding somewhere inside it—exerted some kind of mental force over her.

Ridiculous, she told herself. Were Caine and Gabriel's fantasies contagious? Her rational mind insisted that she had stayed with them because she wanted to. And she planned to return in a few hours for the same reason.

Just to be on the safe side, she punched the gas and doubled her speed. The nervous feeling faded along with her view of the house as it dropped behind the veil of trees.

A ribbon-thin road took her through the woods, along the treacherous edges of steep ocean-side cliffs, and past dark, overgrown bogs that looked ready to gulp down careless travelers. Thankfully, her GPS came back on about forty-five minutes into her quest. It guided her to a remote but numbered highway, and from there to a small village that made Darkisle look like a bustling metropolis. A line of quaint shops lined the single main street, and beyond that lay a few rows of modest homes with SUVs, trucks, and other rough-terrain vehicles parked outside them. Lindsay almost wept to see that the collection of shops included a Laundromat, a general store with a gas pump, and a restaurant featuring a faded sign shaped like a coffee cup.

She headed to the Laundromat first, tossed in a load of clothes, then hit the coffee shop for a restorative infusion of caffeine, grease, and cholesterol. Afterward she spent some time browsing the general store, selecting a few staple items and some produce from a grocery section in the back. To compensate for the fattening breakfast she'd wolfed down, she decided to concoct a healthy stir fry for her evening meal. Maybe she could even entice Caine and Gabriel to share some. She was convinced they kept a secret stash of ordinary food somewhere, allowing them to maintain their vampiric fast in the main areas of the house. Her best guess was the locked basement she'd discovered the day before. She wouldn't be surprised to find an entire apartment set up downstairs, with all the modern conveniences and hideaways for the guys besides. If only she could steal a glimpse ….

The middle-aged woman behind the counter eyed her with undisguised curiosity as she paid for her items. Lindsay suspected they didn't get a lot of tourist traffic up here, the rack of moose-stenciled t-shirts notwithstanding.

"On vacation?" the woman asked while she counted out the change.

"Yes," Lindsay answered, amazed at how smoothly fibs rose to her lips these days. A devious idea struck her. "I'm renting an old place up on the cliffs. It needs some work, but I'm making progress. My problem is that a few of the door locks are rusted. I can't get into the root cellar at all. I don't suppose you sell some kind of skeleton key that would fit an old lock from a hundred years ago?"

"I don't, but there's a locksmith down the street," the woman said. "What he don't know about doors and latches and the like'd fit in a thimble. Sells antiques, too. Betcha he could help you out."

Lindsay struggled to suppress her excitement. "Great. Guess I'll head right over."

An hour later, she was back on the road, her duffel full of clean laundry and a brown paper bag from the locksmith on the seat beside her. She doubted the lock picks he'd sold her were strictly legal, but apparently plenty of his customers inherited old houses, trunks, and desks whose keys had long ago vanished or broken. He'd become something of an expert in jimmying things open, and after a quick lesson in the shop, she felt confident enough to experiment for herself.

Granted, the ethics of the situation presented a sticking point. Breaking into the basement wasn't the best way to repay the guys for their hospitality, but Lindsay was beginning to lose patience with their constant need to surround themselves with mystery. Not only would a glimpse at their presumed hiding place provide her with information she could use in her research, the knowledge would allow her to come to terms with the feelings she'd developed for them.

Because she'd meant what she'd told Caine. With time, she did believe that the emotional connection the three of them shared could turn into something meaningful. Pretending to be vampires had been more exotic and exciting than she'd anticipated, and both men acted their roles to perfection. At some point, though, they'd all have to move forward, and when the time came for a serious discussion, Lindsay wanted to be prepared.

The GPS blinked off again as she approached the familiar gravel road, but she'd had the foresight to memorize a series of landmarks that led her back to the house without too much difficulty. Another unexpected sensation washed over her as she pulled into the driveway, but this one proved more pleasant—as if she were coming home.

Her mood brightened as she carried her purchases inside. A few more hours, and the three of them would spend another evening together. Already the flesh along her spine and between her legs was tingling in anticipation of the pleasures they might bring her tonight. Perhaps they'd stroll out to the gazebo again—and this time Gabriel would finish what he'd started the night before.

She stashed the laundry back in the guestroom, added a few logs to the fire in the sitting room hearth, and then laid out the vegetables and spices on the kitchen counter. As she began to chop, she brooded over the issue of the basement door. Finally, she left everything to marinate and went up to her room for the pick she'd bought in the village. She saw no harm in fitting it into the lock to see if it worked. Afterward, she could abandon the whole scheme if that seemed best.

The antique mechanism resisted her efforts at first. A tangle of corroded iron parts and worn springs clicked and squealed as she pried at them with the tool. Soon the heavy door gave a moan of surrender and swung open.

Right away, her hopes faded. A narrow flight of stairs led not to a secret bachelor pad, but to a dark, windowless root cellar. She groped for a light switch, found one, and snapped it on. An eerie red light bathed two curtained platforms at the rear of the cavernous space. Could these be their beds?

Lindsay moved quietly across the room and gingerly moved the first curtain aside. Sure enough, Caine lay on a low, platform-style inclusive look in hopes of spotting an obvious hiding place for the key. Most promising was a coat rack set up between the two beds. Caine's outfit from the night before hung on a peg, along with a dressing gown. Gabriel treated his clothes haphazardly, dropping them on the ground beside his bed. Lindsay knelt and went through those first, checking all the pockets and inside folds but finding nothing. Next, she moved to the coat rack and went through Caine's garments inch by inch. His pockets, too, proved empty, even the small hidden ones inside the dressing gown. Every now and then, she stole a furtive glance at their sleeping forms, but detected no movement.

When the clothing failed to yield anything useful, she began to search other areas of the basement for a peg, a niche in the wall, or even a toolbox stashed in a corner. The red lighting made it difficult to see, and groping along the walls with her hands made her nervous all over again. She imagined all sorts of hideous creatures skittering away from her in the darkness.

"You have to get a grip," she reminded herself out loud. To put things in clinical terms, this was beyond crazy. Going undercover to research sexual fetishes was one thing. Having three-way sex with, and then trying to loot the tomb of, two vampires was totally off the scale. Yet the dread of what they might do to her when they woke up kept her focused on her task in spite of its outward absurdity.

Stymied, she returned to the bottom step and sat for a while, trying not to tremble in despair. The only spots left to search were the beds themselves—each one containing a slumbering vampire. How much time had passed since she'd so stupidly locked herself in here? For all she knew, they might already be on the verge of waking up.

She had no choice. Biting her lip to steady herself, she approached Caine's bed first. Her fingers went numb as she grasped the edge of his silk sheet and peeled it back, exposing his nude body.

Was she totally depraved? Even now, she couldn't help but feel a twinge of desire as she looked at his muscular frame stretched out before her. The red light washed the planes and curves of his muscles in an interesting mix of shadow and scarlet, making him resemble an erotic painting or photograph. Though he might be in an altered state just now—to say the least—this was still the man to whom she'd given herself, in ways she could never have imagined a few days earlier. As she looked at him, her fear gradually gave way to a more conflicted play of emotions, one of which resembled an urge to protect him.

But maybe that, too, was the result of the vampire spell he'd talked about before, when she'd foolishly chosen not to believe him. She'd have to rethink a lot of what he'd told her.

Kneeling, she slid her palms between the mattress and the bedframe, then between the sheet and the mattress. She repeated the process on Gabriel's bed and sheets. Still nothing.

Tears of frustration rose to her eyes. The key had to be here somewhere! The two of them unlocked the door from inside every night. They'd keep the key in a place that was both accessible to them and not too obvious to an intruder—like her—in case of emergency. What was she missing?

Could it be taped to Caine's skin somewhere? Her gaze traveled again over his sleek, naked body—not an entirely unpleasant task. He didn't have many hiding places to choose from, and he wasn't wearing a necklace, bracelet, or even an anklet. She remembered that his pillow had fallen to the floor—that was a place she hadn't thought to check, since it had dropped between the bed and the wall, out of sight.

In order to retrieve the pillow, she had to crawl onto the bed, lean over Caine's shoulder, and reach between the mattress and the wall. When she hauled it up, she thought she saw a tiny object move inside the pillowcase. Quickly she turned the whole thing upside down and shook it.

A hand shot out and closed around her wrist like an iron manacle. Her breath caught in her throat and her heart came to a complete stop as Caine sat up.

"Lindsay." He spoke her name in a near-whisper. "What a charming sight to wake up to."

He was holding her tightly enough to crush the circulation in her hand. Her fingers grew numb and cold, like they did when she fell asleep with her arm tucked underneath. Then he smiled, his long fangs glinting, and the veins in the rest of her body slowly turned to ice.

Chapter 10

As Lindsay's alarm grew, Caine's lascivious grin widened. "Since you're here, we might as well make the most of it. Take off your clothes."

Lindsay blinked back anxious tears. "Please don't force me."

"You draw the line at joining me in my tomb? Fine, I respect your human taboos. Cultural relativity shall prevail. Anyway, it must be nearly dusk. We'll discuss this upstairs."

His hand slid from her wrist. Lindsay nervously rubbed the warmth back into her fingers.

Meanwhile, the curtains of the other bed began to shake as Gabriel roused himself. He lay propped on his right elbow, blinking at the two of them in surprise. "What's going on? Why is Lindsay down here?"

"An excellent question. One I hope we can resolve with a minimum of unpleasantness."

Without looking at her, Caine retrieved his dressing gown. Gabriel got up slowly, his movements groggy and stiff. His face registered bewilderment as he pulled on his jeans and shirt.

"You're a mess," Caine barked at him. "You need to feed."

"When I'm ready," Gabriel retorted. Lindsay shot him a nervous glance, but didn't dare to speak further in front of Caine, who motioned for her to precede them upstairs.

She walked into the room where she had first seen the painting. Her naïveté amazed and embarrassed her all over again. Why hadn't she realized the portrait's significance the moment she'd discovered it?

Caine held up the lock pick, which he'd pulled from the door. Gabriel followed him into the room, his mouth open in surprise. "Would you care to explain this now?"

Lindsay took a deep breath and pushed onward, hoping she sounded more confident than she felt. "Okay, I admit I broke into the basement. I'm curious about the way you live and where you spend the day. I wanted to see for myself."

"I should have realized a locked door would serve as a magnet for you." Caine sighed. "In a way, I admire you for daring to go against our wishes. But the larger question remains—why are you so curious? You are unlike any donor I've ever used, even the new ones. You give yourself to us, yet you hold back in a way I have not experienced before. You find as much pleasure in disobeying us as you do in serving us." He moved closer until the coldness of his body permeated her skin. "What do you want from us, exactly?"

The flippant answer she'd prepared died on her parted lips. Both Caine and Gabriel scrutinized her face, ready to pounce on even the slightest deception. Under these circumstances, she had no right to expect leniency.

The moment had arrived, she realized. They had to get everything out in the open. In time, Caine would uncover her identity and figure the rest out himself. Far better for the truth to originate from her.

She drew a calming breath that didn't quite have the desired effect. "All right. I guess I do need to come clean with both of you. I can't see our relationship—whatever it is—surviving without honesty. And I want it to survive."

Caine turned an accusatory gaze on Gabriel. "I told you something else was going on with her. You didn't care to listen."

Gabriel stepped between them, his arms spread like a shield. "Why don't you give her a chance to explain? Everything's always about you, Caine."

"Because I'm the one protecting us both. You don't seem to care whether we remain safe or not."

Lindsay ignored their bickering. "I need to tell you more about the way I found you, the reasons I came to you, and why I stayed here with you."

"Go on." Gabriel's voice was steadier than Caine's, less angry, but she still detected an underlying agitation.

She chose her words carefully. "You already know I came to Purgatory to learn about vampires, and to become part of their—or I guess I should say your—culture. What you don't know is that my original goal wasn't sexual gratification or…feeding. At first, I just wanted to observe."

"That's not a big deal," Gabriel said. "Plenty of donors start out the same way. They're afraid to take that final step. You're glad you did, aren't you?"

"Yes, yes, of course I am. But my case is more complicated. You see, I also wanted to write about what I had seen—about vampires."

"I asked you if you were a journalist," Caine snapped. "You told me you weren't."

Gabriel flashed him a disdainful smile. "So she actually managed to lie right to your face, Caine. What a blow to that legendary self-esteem."

"No," she assured them. "I told the truth. I'm not a journalist or a professional ghost-hunter. My interest in vampires was academic, or so I told myself. Once I got to know you, obviously, other considerations arose. Complications."

"Explain."

"I'm a graduate student in psychology, about to earn my doctorate. All I needed to do was find an interesting dissertation topic, something my committee would consider relevant and original enough to approve. I really did hear about your club from some people in my high school. I spent a whole year tracking down the location of Purgatory. I decided to start my research by infiltrating the crowd."

"Your intention was to study vampires," Caine surmised with growing outrage. "Like animals in a zoo? Or perhaps I should say a laboratory?"

"More like an anthropological expedition."

"Dangerous," Gabriel murmured.

"I ignored the danger because I refused to believe you were real vampires. The scientist in me considered that impossible. I believed the whole blood-drinking thing was just a game—a sexual fetish, which I intended to study. I played along, rejecting every piece of evidence that didn't fit into my preconceived theory. " Her eyes dropped in humiliation. "It took me a while to realize I was fooling myself."

"So staying with us was an experiment," Gabriel said. He still sounded more hurt than angry, but she suspected his mood could change quickly. "You wanted to gather information."

"Yes. At first, I did think of it that way. We were all consenting adults, I thought. Why not? I'd been alone for so long. And I definitely enjoyed it. The sex, the biting, everything went way beyond what I imagined." She swallowed. "I mentioned the man I loved in college. He was the one who took me to the medieval party I told you about. I thought we were completely in tune. Then he left me because I wasn't sexually adventurous enough. I never recognized that he was the problem, not me. I guess part of me has always wanted to prove him wrong."

"At least you succeeded in that," Gabriel mumbled. He rubbed a hand over his face, hiding his expression from her. She had to guess at his reaction, but Caine's was plain enough. His cheeks were gaunt and pale, but his eyes blazed. He was on his way to full-blown fury.

He pressed in closer. "And now all that remains is for you to betray us."

"If betrayal were my intention, would I be telling you this now? I could just wait until tomorrow, when the two of you are resting, and slip away. Or I could have brought some sharp implements into the basement with me." She lifted her head and faced him. "Neither ever occurred to me, because I've come to care about you, Caine. I hope you can believe that, even if you discount everything else I've ever said to you. I swear it's the truth."

"You forget that I can prevent you from harming us. As for your spontaneous confession, I too enjoy some expertise in human psychology, though I gained mine through practice and not in a classroom. I know guilt can affect humans strangely. And I am not easily manipulated."

"This isn't about manipulation. Yes, I deceived you, and I regret that. But what matters is that the three of us found one another. You'd think after studying the human mind for so long, I'd be more in touch with my own needs. I wasn't, though. You and Gabriel changed my life...changed me."

"How touching." The words vibrated with sarcasm.

At last, Gabriel spoke. She couldn't interpret the emotion behind his flat, indifferent tone. "So what are you planning to do with the information you've gathered?"

"Nothing. My original hypothesis was wrong. You're not playing a game or indulging a delusion. I realize things exist in this world that I have no concept of, much less any right to interpret." She shrugged, though the gesture didn't come off as casual as she'd hoped. "Besides, if I did tell anyone at the university what I'd discovered, they'd laugh at me. Professors tend to avoid subjects that defy rational analysis."

"Nonetheless, someone might become intrigued," Caine decided after a moment of thought. "It's a chance we cannot take. We must protect ourselves first, as always."

"You mean you'll do to her what you did to Piletta." Gabriel turned to Lindsay and noted her puzzled expression. Nostrils flaring in rage, he stormed to the closet and pulled the portrait back out. He held it front of himself like a shield, shaking the frame for emphasis. "We never finished telling you about the woman in the painting. I'd hoped Caine would possess the courage to admit what he did. Then again, I can understand why he's ashamed."

"I have nothing to be ashamed of," Caine retorted. "I did what I had to do. It's high time you accepted it."

"All right, if you're so convinced your actions were justified, tell her the whole story."

Lindsay looked from one of them to the other. Both of their expressions had turned stubborn and angry. "Tell me what? Caine...?"

"He'll never tell you," Gabriel scoffed, propping the picture against the wall and crossing his arms. He looked from Lindsay to the painting and finally at Caine. "Piletta shared this home with us once, just as you're doing now. Until Caine killed her, that is."

"Oh." A cold sweat snaked down her spine. Lindsay swallowed hard. She should have seen this coming, all of it. Why had she gotten so caught up in her feelings for them? She'd turned into the exact sort of clueless, delusional creature she'd once suspected them of being. Caine, at least, was capable of the most extreme forms of violence. Gabriel might be, too, for all she really knew about him. "Are...are you planning to kill me, too?"

"No." Caine made a slashing motion through the air in front of him. "But I can fix things so that your memories of us...and Purgatory...disappear."

"Caine, no!" Gabriel shouted. "You can't do that!"

"Obviously, I can. And I must. Surely you wouldn't prefer the alternative."

"If you wipe her memory, she'll never be the same person again."

"That's the idea, you fool."

"But you'll change her personality," Gabriel continued to argue. "Everything she's done and learned these past few days will be gone. It'll be like she never met us!"

"Exactly."

"Well, I happen to like her the way she is." Caine sighed as Gabriel took a step backward, positioning himself in front of Lindsay. "I can't let you do it, Caine."

"You honestly have no sense of self-preservation, do you? If it weren't for me—"

Before Caine finished speaking, Gabriel's right hand shot out and seized the front of his robe. A powerful twist of his arm sent Caine sprawling onto the floor. In a flash, Caine rolled back onto his feet, ready for combat. With a feral snarl, Gabriel dropped into a crouch and then sprang forward again.

Their battle unfolded almost too quickly for Lindsay to follow. Her eyes registered little more than a blur as they fought their way across the room, locked in a deadly embrace.

As they scuffled, Lindsay felt her own muscles tense and her combat instincts sharpen. Common sense told her to run, hide, do anything to distance herself from them and their plans for her. Yet the emotion surging through her now didn't seem like fear. Instead, she savored both the rush of adrenalin and a strange invincibility that swelled in her veins. Was this what Gabriel had referred to earlier, when he'd promised that nourishing them would make her stronger, too? No, she wouldn't flee.

They hit the wall together, Gabriel's shoulders crashing into the exact center of the portrait. Lindsay heard a splintering sound, and several jagged shards of wood flew at her.

When Gabriel staggered upright, he was holding the horizontal section of the frame. The broken tip at the end formed a perfect stake.

Caine recognized its significance at the same instant Lindsay did. He drew himself into the corner, raising both arms in front of him. His ragged intake of breath betrayed his alarm.

Gabriel prowled to the opposite side of the room, wielding the makeshift stake like a rapier. A single flick of his wrist thrust it directly into the heart of the fireplace and touched it to the last remaining clump of embers. The dry antique wood ignited at once.

In the end, he didn't turn it on Caine.

He turned it on himself.

"I can end this right here. The fire will destroy me at last. The remnants of my body can follow my soul into oblivion."

"Put it down." To Lindsay's surprise, Caine stepped up to protect her. He moved sideways, shielding her with his own body. "You'll take the house with you—including me and Lindsay."

"My quarrel isn't with Lindsay. Tell her to run. This is between us."

He held the burning wand out to the side and tilted it so. Orange flames crept down its length and curled around his fingers.

The process was slow, agonizingly slow, not at all the way an ordinary man would burn. Lindsay watched with horror as the intense heat turned the skin on his hand a feverish red, then black. The loose cuff of his sleeve began to burn next, the thin cotton flaring and flaking away like chips of old paper. Through it all Gabriel watched himself smolder, his gaze distant and hypnotic, his jaw clenched in determination.

The brief flash of courage she'd experienced before now flared as strong and thick as the flame devouring Gabriel's hand. Pushing Caine aside, she approached the growing conflagration. Her insane confidence startled her more than it did them.

"Gabriel, don't hurt yourself," she pleaded. "Or Caine. He cares about you more than you know."

"He has a fine way of showing it. He just decided to wipe your memory." Gabriel's voice was steadier now, almost disembodied. Fire had engulfed his entire hand, making her wonder how he continued to cling to the stake. His fingers withered and began to shrink under the onslaught. Still, his grip never loosened.

"We can figure our next step out later. For now, please put the fire down."

He seemed not to hear her. "Do you realize how many times over the last century I've walked out on the cliffs and thought about jumping? But why bother? Nothing would happen to me. I could shatter myself on the rocks, wash away in the tide, and moments later I'd be whole again. Can you understand how that feels? Without death, what meaning can life have?"

"Mine has meaning," Caine said. "Yours does, too, Gabriel."

"I wish I could agree." Gabriel paused, his face twisting into a hideous grimace as the fire penetrated to the next level of his body. They didn't have much time.

Briefly, his gaze strayed to the crumbled remains of the painting.

"I understand you still blame Caine for what happened with Piletta," Lindsay improvised. "He had a reason for what he did, though. Maybe if you let him explain—"

"She is correct," Caine admitted grudgingly. "There are things about her I've never told you."

"I know more than you think I do." Gabriel's voice cracked as he fought back tears. "I'm aware that she wanted to destroy me. I didn't care. In fact, I wanted her to. I even encouraged her to fall in love with you, so you and she could move on without me. Why did you stop her?"

Astonishment rendered Caine temporarily speechless. Recovering, he took a hesitant step closer. Lindsay knew the fire had the ability to destroy him, too. His simple act had required immense courage.

"Because I wanted you to live much more than I ever wanted her, Gabriel." He spoke rapidly, but emphatically. A few more seconds would make it impossible to stanch the flame now licking halfway up Gabriel's forearm. "I brought you into this existence because I wanted you to live forever. I thought you—and your talents—were worth preserving." He held out his own hand. "Perhaps I was foolish, even selfish, but I still believe in you. This is home, Gabriel. Lindsay and I are here to share it with you. Give us that chance."

"No," Gabriel groaned. The fire crackled, devouring another section of his arm in a flash of acrid-smelling heat. "You killed Piletta. You'll kill her, too, and we'll just be in the same place again."

"No harm will come to Lindsay," Caine vowed. "I give you my word."

His jaw remained clenched, his fangs gritted. Lindsay could see that he was acting against his better judgment. His concern for Gabriel's well-being, however, overrode his distrust of her. In truth, she was as much relieved for herself as for him. She had no doubt that Caine had intended to follow through with his mind-wiping threat.

"Your word? What a joke." Gabriel attempted a sardonic laugh, which came out as an agonized moan. Lindsay gasped as his undead skin began to pucker and peel away from his wrist and elbow, revealing a core of black, desiccated tissue.

"In spite of our differences, I think you would be hard-pressed to identify a single instance of duplicity on my behalf." Caine moved closer, reaching for the torch. The fingers that grasped it had grown nearly skeletal, the joints connecting them little more than ash. Any moment, they would drop away and leave the fire to spread wildly over the rest of Gabriel's body and the room. "I want you to survive, Gabriel," he said. "We both do."

"And what good is that, when I don't want to survive myself?"

His hand moved, and the flame hovered closer. Lindsay smelled both burning cloth and flesh.

Chapter 11

Caine lunged like a streak of lightning and reached through the fire to snatch Gabriel's weapon away. He held the torch aloft, his own flesh darkening from even the brief exposure to the intense heat, and unleashed a terrifying snarl of anguish. In the instant before the flame latched onto him, he flung the offending instrument back into the fireplace. The blazing hunk of wood clattered behind the grate and faded to an innocuous glow.

Gabriel's hand and arm, however, remained alight. Thinking fast, Lindsay snatched the quilt from the floor. She flung it over his shoulder, grabbed him around the waist, and squeezed her body as tightly to his as she could. She was able to smother the flames in seconds, thanks to the thickness of the quilt and her own swift, determined actions. When at last she felt the deadly heat subside between them, she sagged against Gabriel in relief. He hissed in pain as he slid his uninjured arm around Lindsay's shoulders and embraced her. As they clung to one another, the tension ebbed from his muscles and his labored gasping slowed.

A new sensation startled her. She looked up to find that Caine had placed a hand on each of their backs. Leaning close, he eased them apart. The quilt, blackened with soot but otherwise undamaged, slid to the floor and covered their feet.

"A most impressive effort," Caine complimented her. "You are a woman of many hidden talents, Lindsay."

"Girl scout training," she explained. "First time I've ever used it. I'm glad it worked."

"Show me your arm," he demanded of Gabriel, who offered his destroyed limb without protest. Lindsay averted her eyes as Caine skimmed back the paltry remains of his sleeve and examined the wound. She didn't care to look at what lay beneath the crumbled garment. She imagined she would see scorched tissue, seared all the way to the bone. Though she doubted vampires were prone to infection, such severe damage would require treatment of some sort.

Along with fire safety, she'd also received rudimentary instruction in First Aid. However woefully insufficient her skills, she felt compelled to offer Gabriel whatever small comfort she could. Steeling herself against the gory spectacle that awaited her, she turned back toward Caine and peered over his shoulder.

What she saw shocked her far more than any tangle of bloody sinews and blackened bone. Gabriel's arm had indeed been scorched all the way through, but somehow, defying both logic and biology, the entire limb was already well on the mend.

"I'm sure I don't have to tell you how foolish that was," Caine was saying, turning Gabriel's wrist over in his own hands. Lindsay gaped as the charred skin swelled, lightened in color, and flowed upward to cover the lacerations. "Even vampire physiology has its limits."

"I…think I…made my point," Gabriel replied in a strained voice. "Lindsay will be…safe now."

He wrested his arm from Caine's grip and reached for her instead. Lindsay covered his palm with both of hers. She kissed his fingers, marveling at his perfectly restored skin and nails. He squeezed back, testing his strength.

"Isn't she?" he prodded when Caine didn't respond.

"I gave you my word," Caine admitted with a scowl. "I intend to keep it—though I still think you underestimate the threat she poses to us."

"Well, I give you my word that I'll protect your secret," Lindsay said. "I can't see why that isn't good enough."

"I suppose it will have to be...for now."

She searched his face, then Gabriel's. Moments before, she'd been convinced everything between them, including Gabriel himself, was lost. The emotion welling up in her now went far beyond relief. Perhaps she ought to fear Gabriel, and especially Caine, but she didn't. What she did feel toward them was strange, intense, and definitely addictive. She knew that if she lived as long as they had, she would never find it again with any human man...or men. She had no desire to try.

All that remained was for her to put what she felt into words.

"I love you both," she blurted as her own eyes filled with tears. "I want you to love one another again."

Gabriel cautiously extracted his hand, flexed his fingers, and pointed at Caine. "Do you know what your problem is, Caine? It's that you can't love because you can't trust. If you truly want to do something for me...to make my existence bearable again...you'll have to learn how."

Caine's brows shot up. "I don't think I—" he began, then thought better of his response and stopped. "But all right. I'll try."

"We can work with that."

"You ought to get some rest now. Healing can drain a man. Especially when he hasn't fed. May I suggest you take Lindsay with you?"

"I'll feed when I'm ready. Still...Lindsay and I do have some unfinished business upstairs." Gabriel turned to her. "Will you come?"

"Yes," Lindsay said.

"What about you?" Gabriel asked Caine as he and Lindsay, hand in hand, prepared to walk past him.

He stood with his back to them, arms folded, gazing at the crumpled remains of the portrait. "I'll stay down here a while. This room could use some straightening."

"Will he burn it?" Lindsay whispered to Gabriel as they climbed the stairs.

"Hide it, more likely. You heard him blather on about my so-called talent. It's a matter of pride for him. Besides, he's in the picture. He's too vain to destroy an image of himself."

Back in his room, Gabriel stripped naked and crawled onto the bed. Lindsay followed him, shedding her own clothes and kneeling between his legs. Neither spoke as he swept her up in a crushing embrace.

His lips trailed to her neck, his tongue skidding down the pulsing vein that throbbed below her ear. Lindsay tensed, half-expecting to feel his teeth. Instead, he drew his head back and kissed her deeply, sensually. His passion penetrated every fiber of her body. Her own surged in her chest and spread until she ached to pull him inside her. He soon obliged her, positioning her on top of him and bucking his hips so that he entered her in a single, determined thrust.

After the scene downstairs, her emotions were raw, her nerves abuzz. In no time she was coming hard, fast, and long. The orgasm went on and on, sweeping them both away into a few moments of sweet oblivion.

"Caine probably has a point. You should feed. You look exhausted."

"In good time. I'm at peace right now. Telling Caine off was…cathartic. Let me bask in the sensation."

"Okay." Lindsay dozed for a while with her cheek against his chest. She imagined she could hear his heart thudding deep inside him, but soon she realized she was listening to her own. Frowning, she opened her eyes and studied him. Gabriel sensed her interest and stirred.

"What would it take for your life to have meaning again?" she asked, tracing a finger down his rib cage. "I don't mean just tolerable. Your art?"

His face clouded. "I don't know. I haven't painted in so long.…"

Without a shred of shame or hesitation, she rolled away from him and stretched out on the pillows. "Why don't I model for you?"

"Because I don't have paint, for one thing."

"So make a sketch first. Surely you can find a pen in one of the drawers."

"No. It's too late. I can't go back to what I once was."

"Then why not be different? Better? You can reinvent yourself. Maybe you and Caine…and I…can start fresh."

"I said no." He rolled onto his side, away from her, and drew the blanket over himself.

"All right. I didn't mean to pressure you." Stung, she turned from him, too. Before long she was asleep.

She woke some time later to find him sitting up next to her. A candle burned on the nightstand beside him, providing the room's only light. Propped on his knees was an old-fashioned sketchbook. His expression showed intense concentration as his hand sped across the pad.

Suddenly, he flung down his stubby pencil with a curse. "My talent's gone. I can't do it. I shouldn't have tried."

"No," Caine's voice broke in from the darkness. She noticed him then, standing in the shadowed area beside the door. His eyes were trained on what Gabriel had drawn. "You must keep going."

Tears slid down Gabriel's cheeks. His hand trembled, but slowly began moving on the paper again.

"You can do this," Caine said.

"I know."

Epilogue

Five Months Later

Lindsay pulled into the driveway just as the first snowflakes hit the windshield. According to every forecast over the last forty-eight hours, the coming storm promised to be one for the record books. Roads would be impassable for days, trees and buildings were at risk for collapse, and some areas expected to lose power. Every resident for miles around had spent the entire week preparing for the worst.

She, on the other hand, was looking forward to the whiteout. The supplies she'd brought from the village would get her through the ordeal, and Gabriel's house had weathered far worse than a few feet of ice and snow.

She spent the last few hours of daylight putting everything in place, including a few flashlights and candles just in case they did lose electricity. Then she went to the makeshift office she'd set up, turned on her laptop, and tried to get a little work done while she had the house to herself.

The blizzard arrived right on schedule, howling with fury and depositing foot after foot of fluffy white snow onto the grounds. From behind her computer, Lindsay watched it pile up around the windows. She added a few logs to the fire and waited for the men to arrive.

Gabriel came up first, a soft red bathrobe tied loosely around his waist. The robe had been a gift from her, and she never tired of seeing it drape sensually against his bare skin. He held his hands out to her, lifted her and kissed her full on the mouth. "Productive day?"

"Yep. Got five more pages done. My advisor will be amazed when I drive up at the end of the month and drop another chapter on his desk."

"I'm glad we still inspire you," Gabriel said.

"You do. In every way possible." Lindsay slid her palms down his back and squeezed his rear end playfully. In response, his erection snapped up thick and rigid against the crotch of her jeans. True, her dissertation committee had expressed some concern when she'd announced her choice for a final topic—the psychological process of forgiveness—but since then, they'd agreed that she brought a fresh perspective and a lively writing style to the project. If all went as planned, she would have both her Ph.D. and a publishable manuscript by the end of the year. Maybe her new topic wasn't as lurid or exciting as vampire sex clubs, but the significance it held for the three of them made it far more fulfilling than anything else she'd ever studied.

Caine arrived next, his hair and skin fresh with a musky cologne. For a moment, he paused to admire the sight in front of him—Lindsay and Gabriel embracing in the flesh, while above them hung Gabriel's masterful portrait of the three of them. Though the basic composition reflected the original portrait of Caine, Gabriel, and Piletta, the entire mood of this one was different. Rather than an air of suspicion and rivalry, the painting conveyed the strength of their ties to one another. The lines and colors merged in full artistic unity, the bond culminating in their interlocking gazes. If anything, Gabriel's powers as an artist had returned stronger than ever once he took up the brush again.

Noticing him, Gabriel and Lindsay drew apart. Together their eyes followed Caine's to the picture.

"I must admit, I never get tired of looking at that," Caine said.

Lindsay touched Gabriel's face. "I knew you could make this house beautiful again."

"The painting's not the only thing that makes it beautiful," he whispered.

Caine moved between them, and the three embraced. In no time, their robes met her own clothes on the floor, and all three stretched out together. They kept a respectful distance from the fire.

Gabriel entered her first, her aroused body welcoming him at once. Deeply imbedded, he rolled onto his back and nestled her on top of him. Caine knelt between Gabriel's legs and slipped his arms around Lindsay's waist. His cool lips trailed over her left shoulder, then her right, then drifted to the familiar site on the side of her throat. Her pulse pounded like a lusty drumbeat in her ears. Its insistent hammering stirred his passions, too.

His erection stroked the creamy plane of her backside, keeping perfect time with Gabriel's rhythm inside her. Soon his hands reached to cup her breasts, his thumbs massaging the contracting points of her nipples. Sparks of pleasure zigzagged through her, spiraling like fireworks. Lindsay locked her legs around his hips and rocked her torso back and forth to the beat of her lust-crazed heart, keeping the pace steady.

They'd learned to recognize and react to the sounds she made at various stages of gratification. When she gasped, Gabriel pumped faster and harder underneath her. In no time, the rush of orgasm began, flowering wet and hot between her legs and rapidly spreading outward. Caine finished her off by dropping one of his hands to the moist curls between her thighs. His fingers encircled the sensitive pearl hidden there, coaxing her excitement to the surface.

Lindsay arched her back and moaned as Caine's teeth pierced her flesh, swiftly and painlessly drawing her life into him. His bite, and his suckling, only intensified her enjoyment. Her body went limp, her mind blissfully quiet. Caine held her against his chest as he fed, the pressure of his hands on her sweet spots gradually subsiding.

After a moment or two, he pulled away and switched places with Gabriel. The two of them moved in perfect synchronicity, their actions choreographed by five wonderful months' worth of similar scenes. This time Gabriel drank and Caine used his cock to satisfy her. Whether he brought her to a second climax, or guided her through a series of delightful aftershocks, she was too giddy to tell for sure. What she did know was that the two of them left her lightheaded and shuddering with the perfect combination of sensations.

They rested together, limbs entwined, one man on either side of her. She relaxed into their renewed warmth, happy and protected.

"Oh, I meant to tell you both something. I picked up my mail when I went into town earlier. I've received a wedding invitation from my old friend Briana in Darkisle. She's getting married to some rich guy this summer. I could hardly believe it."

"And this concerns us why?" Caine asked sleepily.

"It concerns you because I was hoping you would be my dates—both of you. Darkisle doesn't get much excitement. We can give them something to talk about. And you don't have to worry. The ceremony starts at night. I thought it might be nice to take a little trip together. We can work out the details later."

"Sounds like fun," Gabriel said. "Maybe they'll commission me to paint a wedding portrait."

"Great idea," Lindsay agreed. She curled against the two of them, closed her eyes, and listened to the storm rage outside. In contrast, their unconventional living arrangement continued peacefully.

Would that tranquility last until Briana's wedding? Lindsay had no way of knowing. She—and they—could only forge ahead one step at a time. Fortunately, Lindsay Tanner, soon to be Dr. Lindsay Tanner, considered herself nothing if not adventurous.

THE END

www.CassandraPierce.com

ABOUT THE AUTHOR

Cassandra Pierce has been a fan of Gothic literature for most of her life, even studying the origins of the genre in college and graduate school. Before long, she got the urge to create paranormal romances of her own and is now hard at work on the third Darkisle novel (among other projects). When she is not writing, she teaches English (including a course on Vampire Lit) at a small New England college and is active in a charity that rescues and rehomes abandoned pets.

Read more about Cassandra's upcoming books at www.CassandraPierce.com, and visit her on Facebook!

Also by Cassandra Pierce

Siren Classic: Darkisle 1: *Heirs to Darkisle*
PolyAmour: Terran Border Patrol: *Captain Gareth's Mates*

Available at
BOOKSTRAND.COM

Siren Publishing, Inc.
www.SirenPublishing.com

Breinigsville, PA USA
16 February 2011
255683BV00004B/199/P